Guilty Pleasures

Sometimes,
it feels good
to be bad...

Lady Jane Sinclair

ISBN: 978-1-60414-982-1

A special thank you to Fideli Publishign for cover creation and book consultation.

For information, please contact
Fideli Publishing, Inc.:
info@fidelipublishing.com

www.FideliPublishing.com

It's All About the Money

Lilly

Becoming an escort was the only decision Dr. Lilly Peters could find that made everything in her life work the way it had to. It paid the bills and kept her grandmother comfortable.

She'd never forget her first encounter. They met at a small hotel in Chicago. Lilly was a little tired from being in the ER all day, but when she stopped for an espresso, she knew she'd be okay. *Thank God for Starbucks!*

As she sat sipping her coffee, she noticed an attractive guy giving her the eye. He was a little older than her, but he was extremely nice looking. He had blonde hair, bright blue eyes and was built like an Adonis. He looked like he might've just come back from a vacation because his skin had a healthy sun-kissed glow.

When he finally got brave enough to approach her, she learned his name was Nick. He didn't talk much, but Lilly was fine with that. What she had in mind for him didn't require much conversation.

They went back to his hotel room, and he seemed a little nervous. "Would you like some wine, dear?" he asked timidly.

He has such a charming voice; maybe he should talk more. "No, thank you. I think I'd rather have you." She was totally out of her comfort zone, but it was also kind of exciting.

Should I talk or just get undressed? Maybe this isn't for me. I should leave and forget this night ever happened. I can't be an escort. I don't feel sexy enough. The doubts ran through her mind until she noticed the way he was looking at her. The hunger in his eyes sent a signal straight to her core.

She went to him and kissed him lightly. He responded immediately and they continued to kiss until they both relaxed. She took his hands and led them to the buttons on her blouse. He deftly followed her unspoken instructions then took the initiative and unhooked her bra. His hands were gentle, and she noticed the color of his eyes had deepened with lust.

Lilly took a few deep breaths and regained control. *How can I be so turned on by someone I don't even know?*

Apparently he felt the same way, because he pushed her down on the bed, raised her legs and took off her panties in one smooth movement. She could feel his warm breath and searching tongue as he began exploring her body. *He's hardly touched me yet, and I can't believe how wet I am.*

"You're so very beautiful," he whispered.

She was still a little cautious, but wanted more. He switched his focus to her breasts, and as he circled her nipples with his rough fingers, she could feel them harden. *He wants me, and I defiantly want him.*

Then, he was on top of her, and immediately inside her. She was on fire, and he was perfect. *This is so much better than I ever imagined! How can being with a stranger be so sensual?*

There was something special about that first secret tryst. She'd never shared a bed with someone she didn't know. It was a thrill and an incredible high. *I'm in! This escort thing is definitely something I can do.*

***

Her men loved surprises and she gave it to them, full force. Just thinking about it made her hot. Imagining what she could do to them was a great aphrodisiac.

Lilly's favorite place to start was in the shower. She turned her anxieties into an asset there, and her confidence drove her clients wild with desire.

First she would lather her partner with a sweet-smelling fragrance — one she liked, and she made sure she used a unique scent for each man. She enjoyed the fact that her lovers were different. Even though this was just a job, she wanted to feel some excitement, not just be a mannequin lying on a bed.

Many times her clients weren't anything like their real world personas when they were with her. This was probably good, because it meant she was providing something they couldn't get elsewhere. The men Lilly had sex with seemed to be searching for something to make them feel better. In response to that need, she was a kind and generous lover who worked to make them believe they were special. She usually succeeded, and they came back for more.

She didn't classify herself as a hooker; she was an escort who only saw the top echelon of men. They paid big bucks to be with her, and she gave them their money's worth every time. Chicago was her playground and it was filled with men who wanted her services.

When they were together, she'd remove her clothes and theirs, and then they'd move to the shower. She'd start with luxurious, therapeutic water play that began with her sensually lathering herself while the client watched.

The man of the evening would be treated to the sight of her hands slowly caressing every part of her body. Some of her men had never been with a woman other than their wives, so taking things slowly to start with was almost required. This little performance did two things — it made the men relaxed and raring to go, and it turned Lilly on like nothing else. By the time she'd finished lathering herself and was ready to start on them, the men were hers to direct any way she liked.

Once she rinsed herself off, it was their turn to do the lathering. She would make sure they touched her in all her favorite places. She had no problem guiding them, and they had no problem accepting her assistance. *They always get harder when they see I'm excited. That's what makes me one of the best — I know this and I always make sure it happens. Not only do they get a good lay, but they also get a woman with style.*

On occasion, a man couldn't seal the deal — either because he didn't truly want it to or because he wasn't ready for the next step. Lilly didn't worry too much when this happened. Frequently, within a week or so, the man in question would be back and ready to rock and roll, requesting repeat performance of her shower treatment. *Eventually, all of my customers leave satisfied,* Lilly thought with more than a little pride.

Lilly especially liked men who leaned her back against the tile in the shower while the water sprayed down on them; it somehow made the experience more seductive. She also enjoyed it when her men kissed and licked her breasts while using their fingers to play between her thighs — first gently, then more aggressively as her passion built. She didn't like to be rushed.

Some of her regulars had figured out exactly what she liked and made sure they gave it to her, including the expensive, shiny baubles she favored. She viewed the jewelry as an insurance policy, and secreted each piece away for use in case of an emergency.

She also found she was easily turned on by a variety of stimuli, and this helped her to be even more successful with her men. She seemed to like different things with different men. Her regulars quickly figured this out and learned that when she was excited, they got a much hotter experience. What they didn't realize was the method to her madness. Lilly didn't actually do much to get them to the euphoric state they craved; she'd just lie back and let them do all of the work. It made them feel powerful and manly, and that helped to make her services even more popular.

She didn't like truly rough sex, and neither did most of her clients. On occasion, she had a request for something she found distasteful, so she would just say no and make sure the man respected her wishes. If a client became too aggressive, she was tough enough to kick him right out of her bed. She would then cross him off her preferred client list.

Pleasing men with money isn't as difficult as I thought. In the boardroom, they might be hard-hitting, cold bastards — but with me, they become my easily manipulated, well-trained pets.

***

Being a doctor was Lilly's dream, and she was living it. *I love it when they call me Dr. Peters!* Her job usually invigorated her, but some days she left the hospital feeling drained. She was having one of those days today and had been on call for what seemed like five days, but it'd really only been 24 hours.

Exhaustion was expected — it went along with the internship territory — but that didn't stop her from trying to unwind before going to sleep. She hated going home to an empty apartment, even though she now lived in a luxury building with a doorman and top security. It bothered her a little that she was still alone when she closed the door, but that wasn't about to change any time soon.

She decided she'd go for a drink after her shift, instead of going straight home. Rather than head to the bar the other doctors hung out at, she went to the only place she knew where she could sit and not be bothered—the bar at the Harrington Hotel on Wacker.

She wasn't much of a drinker, and particularly didn't like drinking alone, but sometimes that was the only way to chase away the bad days. If she wanted conversation, she was on a first-name basis with all of the hotel bartenders. Sometimes they confided in her, but she had yet to reveal anything about herself to them.

Because her father drank too much, even one drink reminded her of everything she'd tried so hard to forget — his smell, his sleeping around with strange women, and his undeniable lack of ambition. Her mother, a pediatric cardiologist, eventually took her own life after several bouts of serious depression that Lilly suspected were connected to her father's behavior.

Having that in her background gave Lilly all the more reason to work hard toward her goal. She was going to be a successful doctor, no matter how difficult it was or how long it took. Her path was there; she just had to follow it and avoid getting pulled into a depression like her mother. *Heredity is not going to dictate who I am. I'm a fighter, not a quitter.*

The Harrington was also where she usually met her clients. She liked how easy being an escort was. Compared to being a doctor and trying to save lives, it was entertaining and she really didn't think of it as screwing for money. Plus, it made her feel good.

Interns were low on the pay scale, so in order to get what she ultimately wanted, she knew she had to work her ass off and do more. If it meant being with men for money, then she was in. The $2000 she got paid for a couple of hours of fun time went a long way in her world. *I like the money and everything it's doing for me. I certainly don't miss being poor.*

Her clients' money also paid for her grandmother's care at a top-level nursing home, which was a godsend. She'd moved her grandmother there after her mother died, and she was now solely responsible for paying for her grandmother's care.

That's really how the whole escort thing had come about. When she'd heard some of the ER doctors talking about a good way to make money on the side, she'd found it impossible not to eavesdrop. That's when she learned about Rayna Rogers. She'd wrangled a meeting with Rayna, and the rest was history. *That's when my life changed for the better. Rayna saved me and became more than just my boss.*

Rayna

Rayna had many of the hospital's interns and residents on her payroll. After meeting with her, Lilly jumped at the chance to earn enough money to get out of her fleabag apartment. She was tired of eggs and toast for dinner, and she hated having to go down the hall to the shared bathroom in her boardinghouse apartment. She was also on the brink of having to give up her dream of being a doctor because she couldn't pay her bills, even though she had scholarships and had landed the internship at Memorial North.

Rayna was good to her "players" as she called them. She explained all the rules to Lilly and, after mulling it over, Lilly accepted. She liked sex, but she never imagined getting paid for it. Money was so tight that she was down to the last of her savings. She knew it was just a matter of time before she'd have to drop out of the program. Ranya's offer was like manna from heaven. In the end, the decision had been easy.

Lilly hailed a taxi on her way to the bar at the Harrington. *It's been a while since I've had a free night. Boy, am I ready!* Since she didn't have a client waiting for her this evening, she knew she could just sit at the bar and not talk to anyone. Doing that seemed so much more appealing than going home alone, even though she was exhausted.

The last thing she wanted was to be alone, not after the day she'd had. Losing three of the eleven patients that came in the ER had been almost more than she could handle. She knew if she went home, she'd probably watch a sad movie or two, eat a bag of potato chips, and feel worse than she already did.

When she got to the hotel, she took her usual seat and sat quietly, watching a guy at the other end of the bar who was watching her. She thought he was gorgeous, and wondered why he was staring at her — she wasn't exactly looking her best. *I don't think I even put on lip-gloss today,* Lilly thought. This was a big deal for her, since she felt like even if she were stranded on a desert island and only allowed to take three things with her; lip-gloss would be one of them. *I don't usually like it when men stare, but the way he's looking at me is kind of hot.*

She was a little surprised she'd even noticed the guy; she rarely looked at men other than her clients. Men liked it when she looked them in the eye while they were screwing or when she was blowing them, but when she was out in public she didn't really look them in the eye. *This guy looks kind of lonely. I wonder why such a great-looking guy is sitting alone in a hotel bar. Maybe he's wondering the same about me.*

The bartender, her buddy Jacob, came up to her and asked, "Your usual?"

"Yep, you got it." She smiled back. Her "usual" meant she'd had a bad day but really didn't want to drink. Jacob would revive her with Irish coffee, holding the Irish. It looked good and stopped unwanted questions. No one wanted to see someone sit at a bar and drink water; it made them feel guilty for drinking.

"Bad day, Doc?"

"Really bad day. Probably my worst in a long time. What about you, Jacob? Didn't you say you were going on vacation?"

"Not happening. My girlfriend broke up with me last night, and I didn't want to go alone. So, I gave my mother and father the tickets and said, 'Hawaii is waiting for you.'"

"Sorry, Jake. I hate it when that happens. At least your parent's will have fun."

Jacob laughed. "I'm sure they will. They've been married for years and still like each other. How about that?"

"Nice to hear someone's happy."

"Bet you've never had someone dump you, Doc."

"You're wrong about that. I've had rough times but look at me I'm here and trying my best to put all the bad stuff behind me."

"Hope I can do that."

"You can. It just takes time."

"Can't seem to shake it."

Lilly smiled. "Truth is I'm still working on it. Crying helped me and I also decided I would never let myself fall in love again — no matter what."

"So, how's that working for you?"

"It's not."

Lilly surprised herself by telling Jacob something so personal. Her cardinal rule was to never talk about anything in her past; now she'd broken it. Hopefully, he wasn't really listening, because she knew he sometimes didn't.

That guy at the end of the bar was still looking at her, which usually made her uncomfortable but not this time. *I wish I looked better this evening,* she mused.

She didn't need to worry though, even without sleep for more than twenty-four hours, she still looked beautiful. Her red hair was neatly piled on her head, with wisps of reddish blonde streaks framing her porcelain face. Her green eyes were unlined and bright, and she had tiny diamond studs in each ear—a gift from one of her men. Simple, but elegant.

Her admirer had deep, compelling eyes; they almost seemed secretive. His hair was black and wavy, and he had olive skin and a charming, but cautious smile. The fact that she didn't know him caused her to fantasize, something she rarely did. *It's too bad I'm so tired...*

After being in the ER for long periods of time, she was more realistic than most. Most of her day was so intense she'd come to believe that if she could share herself and have a man really enjoy her company, it would be a big accomplishment.

She rarely thought of men other than her clients. She wasn't all about fucking, but it did seem that her life was going in that direction. She didn't have lengthy conversations with her clients, but a few shared snippets of their lives with her. On more than one occasion, she felt more like a psychiatrist than an escort.

The only one she shared a little bit of her past with was Rayna, who understood Lilly's situation. Of course, she didn't tell her everything. Rayna was a retired nurse who had needed quick money, so she started her own escort service. At first, it had been slow going, but became easier because she knew many members of Chicago's socialite community through her connections at the hospital. Rayna's new venture was a success that made her a lot of money, and the rest was history.

As the months went on, Rayna wasn't sorry that Lilly put her hospital work first, because there were no client complaints about her services. The two women bonded and had a good working relationship. It also helped that Lilly brought in quite a bit of money. Like most business owners, Rayna wasn't working for the fun of it.

Along with the female escorts, Rayna also had quite a few male employees. Jacob, the bartender, was one of her best. Many of Chicago's successful women had no time for marriage, but needed a good fuck once in a while. Jacob was hot, a good listener and an extremely good lover. He also had a body better than any male model's, and topped it off with an adorable smile.

The female clients loved the fact that he was always so attentive — but it was no secret that if Lilly gave Jacob a chance, he would prefer her to any of them. The only thing was, Lilly had no clue Jacob thought of her this way.

Unexpected Interlude

Just as Lilly was about to call it a night, the stranger from the other end of the bar came and sat down beside her. He handed her a note with his phone number on it that said, "My name is Ben, and I'll be in town for a few days." *I'm tempted but it's not going to happen tonight.*

Lilly didn't know if she should make a fast getaway or sit there and be polite until he got the message. Because she felt a little uncomfortable, there was nothing left to do but leave.

It had been a long time since she'd felt like this, but this guy piqued her interest. Lately, she felt like a sex machine performing on command, but there was still a part of her that could feel alive and energized when a man who wasn't a client showed interest. She was a little excited at the thought of him — this reaction seemed almost too naïve, given her current lifestyle. She didn't like showing too much emotion; she thought it made her seem weak.

On her way out of the bar, she started to think about Ben — his lips, and the intoxicating way he'd smelled. He was sexy. She started to think having him in her bed was what needed to happen. This thought worried her, which was why she was out the door quickly and refused to look back. *I'm an escort, for God's sake. I don't have time to pick up a guy at a bar and take him home, especially if he's not paying. I fuck for money, so no personal life for me. He sure was yummy though...*

When she got outside, she started to throw the note in the garbage, but instead opened her bag and dropped it inside. The fact that there was no last name on the piece of paper meant no promises were implied, just something casual. She could have done casual, but instead she waved for a taxi.

She didn't see Ben behind her as she got into the taxi, so she was surprised when he got in right beside her. She wanted to tell him to leave, but she didn't. Because she said nothing, he stayed. Apparently he knew the night had possibilities.

Neither of them told the taxi driver where to go, so when the cars behind them started honking and the driver could hear people yelling at him, he pulled onto a side street and turned to them. "Either of you have any idea where you wanna go? I'll be happy to sit here and keep the meter running, but you might not like that. So, where to, folks?"

Lilly glanced over at Ben. Just as he was about to kiss her, the driver — who had been watching them in the mirror — turned back toward them and smiled. "Far be it from me to tell my customers what do, but it seems to me like you two need a room. Let me drive you somewhere before my taxi turns into a love nest."

Lilly finally found her voice and told the cab driver, "Park Chicago."

Ben was a little uncomfortable and reluctant to stay, he'd thought this would be a quick fuck and then he'd be gone. He realized he might've made a mistake and things were going to be a bit more complicated than he'd imagined. This wasn't going to be a wham, bam, thank you ma'am type of encounter.

Lilly, on the other hand, wasn't quite sure she was up for having sex with this stranger. *If I'm anonymous, I guess I have nothing to lose,* she reasoned with herself. *Plus, it might help me shed some of the tension from the awful day I've had.* Since Rayna checked out all of her guys before they ever met her, Lilly was a little shocked at herself for deciding to go any further with this guy without knowing he was safe. Ben would be her first pick-up in a long time — but the more she looked at him, the more she wanted him. *I haven't wanted anyone in a long time. He'll certainly do.*

Sitting next to him she felt a warm glow flow through her. A sense of urgency drove her to be bolder than she normally was outside her escort persona.

The more Ben watched Lilly, the more he knew he wanted her. While he knew it was a little crazy to want to be with someone who didn't even give him her name, at this point he didn't really care. He knew he should open the door and get out, but he didn't. There was something so different about this woman. He had to find out more, so he sat back and watched her take charge.

When they got to the hotel, Lilly took out her credit card to pay. Ben, being a gentleman, wanted to do the honors, but she shooed him away. It was obvious she'd done this before.

When they got to the room, there was no conversation. Ben watched as Lilly undressed in a suggestive and stimulating way. She'd learned what pleased her wealthy men, and used it to her advantage. She'd become a seduction expert, but only with paying clients … until now.

Her ease in getting undressed always made men wild. *This is turning me on, especially since he doesn't even know my name. I can rock his world and walk away, and he'll never know what hit him. Wow, this is strange, but I like it!* By this point, she was usually ready for foreplay, but watching Ben become excited was getting her hot. She moaned just thinking about him touching her.

Looking over at him, she couldn't help but wonder who he really was. He was so handsome and had such a charming smile. *Why am I reacting to him like this? It should just feel like he's another john.* She turned on some music and realized Ben was getting hard faster than she'd hoped.

She sauntered toward him, keeping in rhythm with the music. She was still wearing her silky black panties, but they were soaked, and her bare breasts jutted toward him, asking to be touched. As she moved closer, her nipples touched his chest, and she moaned again.

Ben had been with his share of women, but none of them had been like this. It didn't matter to him that he didn't know her; all he seemed to care about was being inside her. He embraced her and moved her toward the king-sized bed. He quickly unbuckled his belt, and Lilly did the rest.

He desperately wanted to lick her nipples, but there wasn't time. Right off the bat, she went for him and had him in her warm, moist mouth in an instant. His breath was coming fast and heavy. The whole experience was such a turn on that he exploded in her mouth and it was all over too fast, like he was some high school kid. He worried that he'd let her down, but she didn't seem to mind.

After a few minutes of her dedicated attention, he was hard again. Not wasting any time, he stood Lilly up and then laid her across the bed. Then, he worked his way up her lovely legs, kissing and licking as he went. When he reached her nipples, he slammed himself inside her. She moaned loudly, which made Ben even more aggressive and he began to ram her with enthusiasm.

The sex was rougher than Lilly normally liked, but for some reason his take charge, Neanderthal possession of her was just what she needed. He pounded into her relentlessly, driving her passion higher and higher. Just when she thought she couldn't take it anymore, he came and she rode the wave right along with him.

Somehow, this night is different. I seem different. I want to stay the whole night with this guy. That hasn't happened since I started working for Rayna. She knew she had to get some rest though; her days were brutally long. Without getting some sleep, she might make a mistake in the ER, and she definitely didn't want that to happen.

Before I leave, I just have to have him one more time — *if he's up for it.* Ben was more than up to the challenge, but after another rousing romp, he promptly fell asleep. *It's time to make my escape. At least he won't be able to track me down.* He'd asked Lilly her name several times during the night, but she never gave him an answer.

She quickly got dressed and tiptoed out of the room, carrying her shoes. *It's better this way.* She didn't know anything about him but his first name and he knew even less about her. *We'll never see each other again, so there's no reason for either of us to know more.* That thought made Lilly sad, and she wondered if she was lying to herself.

As she left the hotel, she stopped at the front desk. Andrew was working. He usually had the late shift, which is why they knew each other well. He was always so nice to her, and she appreciated that.

"Lilly, my dear, how are you? Aren't you staying the night?"

"No, not this time. Can you do me a favor, honey? Please send up my usual breakfast."

"Sure, but it looks like you're leaving."

"Got to. Busy day ahead. "

"I know you love those blueberry pancakes. I'll put your order in for eight as usual. I'll also ask for extra blueberries and powdered sugar. Can I give them a call and set you up in the dining room now, instead?"

"You're so sweet. I wish I could stay."

"You still want me to send up your special breakfast, even though you're not going to be there?"

"Yes, and can you put this note on the tray before it goes to the room?"

"For you, anything."

"Thanks, hon. I owe you. I'll see you soon. Can you do me another favor? Don't give him my name, no matter what. As a matter of fact, don't give out my name to anybody."

"Won't happen. Not on my watch. Your secret's safe with me."

She smiled and waved goodbye. She knew Andrew always had her back. He was one guy she could count on, and the fact that he also worked for Rayna made his promise gold.

***

A Sad but Welcome Windfall

Even before Lilly left her apartment, her phone was buzzing. A text appeared. "We need you." It was the hospital.

"I'm on my way," she texted back. She wasn't on call, but everyone at the hospital knew she'd be there if they needed her. Nothing was as important to her than being a doctor. She lived it every waking moment. She always had the clear message running through her subconscious — *Lives need saving, that's why I'm here.* When anyone was late or didn't show up, she was always first on the call list, and she preferred it that way.

From the moment she got to the ER, she knew it was going to be one hell of a day. There were four shooting victims, several sick kids, and three heart attack patients all waiting for her. She threw on her lab coat, lifted up her hair and twisted it away from her face, then put on a pair of gloves and was ready to begin her day. *I'm glad it's busy; I need to stop thinking about Ben.*

She finally saw her last patient at a little after five. When she was done, she signed out. She had a night on the town planned with Jonah Michaels, her favorite client. He loved coming to Chicago to celebrate his birthday and he always did it with her. He was a successful Texas oil man, and he played that part to the hilt. But with her, he was just an old softy. When he cancelled a two weeks in a row, Lilly asked him if it was his health, but he said he was "tough like a bull" and left it at that. She didn't necessarily believe him, but there was no arguing with him.

He was a great client, and a lot older than most of the men she saw. He was her first repeat client after she started working for Rayna, so he had a special place in her heart. They'd become more like old friends than sexual partners and she'd even told him her real name and daytime profession.

Sometimes, they just talked or went to a movie, even though Jonah liked sex, and was always gentle with her. He was especially considerate of her needs, and usually brought her flowers and candy, which made her feel feminine and less like a machine. On special occasions, he even bought her expensive jewelry, which she kept in a safe-deposit box. *I love his taste in jewelry, especially the beautiful diamond bracelet he brought me last time. Lucky me!*

Her phone rang just as she was about to go home to change, and Jonah's name came up on her screen. "Hey, what's up?" she answered. "You didn't call, so I figured maybe you'd decided not to come."

When he didn't answer, she didn't know what to think. She was just about to hang up when she heard a faint hello. The voice was not familiar.

"Is this Lilly Peters? Dr. Lilly Peters?"

"It is. Can I help you?"

"My name's Miranda. You don't know me, but Jonah Michaels was my dad."

Jonah's dead? Lilly couldn't breathe. Something like this had never happened to her before. She couldn't feel her hands as they gripped the phone. She walked over toward the waiting room in the ER and plopped down on the couch. "What happened? Is there anything I can do?"

She could hear Miranda sniffling from crying. "He had a heart attack and died two days ago. He left a letter for me with instructions to contact you. He wanted me to let you know that his estate lawyer will be calling you to arrange a meeting. He works out of Chicago. My father wanted me to call and personally thank you for consulting with him about his heart condition. He said you helped quite a bit, and he didn't know what he would've done without your advice."

"I'm so sorry for your loss." She held back her tears. "Was he in any pain?"

"It was quick. He just didn't wake up when my mother went to tell him breakfast was ready."

Lilly took a breath. *Married? He always told me he was a widower.* She wanted to hang up the phone and have a good cry, but his daughter obviously wanted to finish what she had set out to say.

"He asked that you use the money he left you to open your own clinic."

Lilly listened without really hearing; her heart was breaking. She hated losing people she cared about. "Money? I don't even know what to say."

"My father didn't usually invest in anything he wasn't sure about. If he left you money he was sure you'd do something good with it, so just say thank you and do what you need to do to make his last wish a reality."

When they hung up, Lilly started to cry. No one had ever done anything like that for her, and she was so thankful. Now all she had to do was get through her internship. She definitely wouldn't use Jonah's money for anything other than what he'd intended. She was grateful, but also so sad that she couldn't thank him in person.

I wonder why he didn't tell me about his heart condition or, for that matter, about his wife. It's too late to be mad at him for that. Besides, knowing him made me a better person. He was a good man. Most men lied in one way or another; that's why I don't trust most of them.

Jackpot!

Her phone rang again and pulled her out of her reverie. It was Rayna. "Hon, can you do me a favor? I know it's not your night, but Lana had to go out of town. I'll make sure you get a bonus."

"Where?"

"The usual. Can you do it, babe?"

"Sure. I just have to go home and change."

Rayna took a breath of relief. "Great. I'll text you the name and particulars."

The bar was unusually busy, and there weren't any tables available when Lilly got there. The text had said, "Dark suit, pink tie." She glanced around the room, and found no one fitting that description. Another text came in. "Sorry, hon. Black suit, gray tie."

There he is. Oh, no! It's Ben! "Oh shit," Lilly mumbled — she hoped not too loudly. She wanted to turn around and walk out, but she froze. He looked even better than he had the night before. *With his looks, I wonder why he needs an escort. I think I'll just leave him sitting there. I hope he hasn't already seen me.*

She wanted to run to him and kiss him as if they were the only two in the room, but that wasn't the case. She wanted to tell him she was sorry she didn't say good-bye or tell him it was a wonderful night for her, but she couldn't. There were so many people in the bar, and she didn't want to make a scene. She wasn't ashamed of what she did for a living; it was just an easy way for her to make money, nothing more.

She watched as Ben waved to a beautiful blonde with long legs and a tiny waist. She looked like she'd just stepped off a magazine cover. She wore a beautiful skin-tight black skirt, a white lace shirt, black-and-white pumps, and a long wrap pearl necklace. The blonde kissed Ben hello, and he seemed happy to see her. So whatever Lilly had been thinking, he wasn't waiting for an escort. Suddenly, he looked at her, but she looked away. In a matter of seconds, she was gone.

Since the client hadn't shown up, she decided to call it a night. She needed to call Rayna to let her know, but she couldn't find her phone. She mentally retraced her steps and then it became clear — she'd left it at the Park Chicago. She'd gone there before coming to the bar. She liked to make sure the room was ready for her client, which always included fresh flowers and soft candlelight. For two thousand a fuck, she didn't want to disappoint.

She went out the door and turned back toward the hotel, and noticed a nice-looking guy wearing a gray tie and black suit was following her.

He called out to her, "Lilly, don't go! Sorry I'm late."

She stopped and smiled. "I thought you weren't coming."

"Good thing Rayna told me how beautiful you were and what you'd be wearing. Otherwise, I'd be lost."

Lilly grinned and shook his hand. "Now that you've found me, you need to introduce yourself. Rayna didn't give me your name. She said you were a friend of hers, and she didn't want to disappoint you because Lana couldn't make it."

"I'm Sam. Can we be honest with each other?"

"Of course. I'd understand if you want to cancel."

"Lilly, I asked for you specifically because I know how wonderful you were to my best friend, Jonah Michaels. He always said what a wonderful doctor you were, and how fond he was of you. I should let you know my full name is Dr. Sam Sheridan."

"Sam Sheridan, the pediatric oncologist? Wow! I've read all your books and papers. You're brilliant." *And I am so lucky. Jackpot!*

"I don't know about the brilliant part. I just know enough to get by."

Lilly smiled. "You're too modest." *Now I'm confused. Is he a client or what?* "Sam, are you here to talk or…?"

"Both, if that's okay."

I think it's more than okay with me! "Come on then, let's go."

They hopped into a cab where Lilly took the lead, "Park Chicago." By the time they got to the hotel, she'd all but forgotten Ben, at least for the time being.

Since Lilly had already checked in, they went directly to the room. When they walked in, the lights were soft and the flowers had given the room a wonderful aroma, just as Lilly intended.

Sam seemed surprised by how romantic everything looked. He wasn't expecting this or the beautiful creature he was with. It was obvious to him how professional and special Lilly truly was.

Sam watched as she started to undress her lean, petite body. She was exquisite, and kept him wanting more by leaving on her bra and panties — suggesting it would be his job to remove those.

As she watched him watching her, she knew he was enjoying himself. *What a great night this turned out to be. I can't believe I'm going to have sex with Dr. Sam Sheridan!*

There was something so attractive about Sam and it elevated her spirit. She decided to let him make the first move, and she didn't have to wait long. He embraced her and kissed her in a romantic way. She wasn't used to this, but she enjoyed it.

The warmth of his breath and the smell of his after-shave immediately aroused her. As she felt his tongue moving down her body, she shivered in anticipation. His hand reached inside her panties and she arched her back to meet it. After a few minutes of his knowledgeable ministrations, she was ready to come. *This is a nice switch. I'm not usually the first to climax.* She'd lost control of the situation, and this time she didn't care. She wanted Sam to keep going. She was holding back, wanting more — making him work for it. Her heart pounded as her body made its way to the grand finale. *Yes! That's exactly what I want. Keep going!*

"Don't stop!" she moaned as his relentless fingers kept up their magic. She knew it was supposed to be her job to make him feel like he'd never felt before, but he'd turned the tables on her. She was so turned on she was panting. She wanted this to last as long as possible, though, so she held on for just a bit longer before her climax crashed over her.

When she'd sufficiently recovered, she slowly unzipped his pants and grasped his substantial manhood. She smiled at his size, and then went down on him like a hungry lioness. He moaned his approval and braced himself so she could reciprocate.

Before she could finish the job, he stopped her and led her to the bed. She kissed him slowly and his excitement grew. When he couldn't stand it anymore, he forcefully took her, and then stopped so she could feel how completely he filled her. She nibbled on his nipples, which drove him wild. He resumed his thrusts, and drove them both over the edge to ecstasy.

When they'd finished, both were sweaty, exhausted and satisfied. Then, Lily did something she'd never done with a client — she fell asleep.

When she woke up, she found an envelope with a note inside it, along with five thousand dollars. She opened the note and read: "Thank you for the beautiful evening. It's one I will never forget." *I wish he'd stayed. I wanted to share my blueberry pancakes with him.*

Truth be told, she was a little upset that Sam left. *I thought we had a connection, but apparently not. I guess it's better this way. I can't care about my clients. That is not a step in the right direction. I know the rules, so what am I doing? Why am I starting to think of the players on my playground as available suitors? I know damn well they're only on loan for the night.*

She closed her eyes and thought about Sam until there was a knock on the door—she'd forgotten to cancel room service. The smell of blueberries filled the room, and then she hoped that she'd see Sam again.

Pleasant Memories

When Lilly got the call from Rayna to meet for dinner at the Black Rose she didn't want to go. It had been one of those days and she just wanted to go home, take a nice long bath and go to sleep.

I've gone out seven nights in a row and I'm sick of everyone. She got that way sometimes. After all, she was stretched pretty thin between the hospital and the escort thing. Being paid to fuck was hard work, but the money was spectacular. *Whoever said you don't need money to be happy must've been rich.*

Not all escorts made as much as Lilly. She was popular, and her men always came back for more, especially Sam Sheridan. Sam was in town every week and he wanted Lilly exclusively; no one else would do. He was strictly a one-woman man, except for his wife, but apparently she didn't count.

Lilly loved their time together. Sam was much more romantic than her other clients. Most of them were rich men who were used to getting their way and didn't want to do anything out of the ordinary — conventional fucking all the way. That's how they referred to it, not her. *Boring!*

Sometimes they just wanted a blowjob and then fell asleep. Lilly considered those bonus days, since she got paid the same amount regardless. These same guys usually added extra cash to her envelope, too. This usually meant she'd treat herself to a shopping spree. *Those tips come in handy and I do love shoes!*

Sam took her places like the opera, museums, and plays. Every so often they even went away for a weekend and stayed at a bed and breakfast in Wisconsin. As she went in to run her bath, she thought back to their last trip.

A limo had picked her up after a rough night in the ER. She was glad Sam hadn't come along for the ride because she got to grab a few hours of sleep and regroup before seeing him. Bad nights in the ER took their toll, and this had been an exceptionally bad one.

By the time she got to the B&B, she was feeling better. Lake Geneva was beautiful, and she was looking forward to a relaxing weekend.

When she got out of the limo, Sam was there, waiting for her. *He's so handsome and I love the way his eyes always light up when he sees me.*

"What do you think?"

"It's so beautiful here. Thank you for always knowing what I need."

"Not a problem, sweetie. Let me show you around."

"It's so peaceful," she said after they'd walked for a while. "Are there a lot of guests this weekend?"

"Nope. It's just the two of us. The staff will make sure everything this wonderful place has to offer is yours for the asking."

Lilly laughed. "You're kidding, right?"

"Nope."

When they went inside, Lilly felt like royalty. There were fresh roses everywhere. Sam knew how much she loved them, so he always had them waiting for her wherever they went.

The entire bed and breakfast was nearly overflowing with roses in every color and variety. It was stunning.

When they got their room, it smelled beautiful. *Everything's perfect. Sam's perfect. It would be so easy to… Remember, Lilly, he's just on loan for a night.*

Sam handed her a fluffy robe, and she decided to put on a show for him before she put it on. She slowly removed each article of clothing until nothing was left but her delicate lacey panties. She knew she was making Sam hard and it made her smile.

Even though he liked it when she took her panties off, she asked him to do the honors this time. He smiled, and slid them off for her after she laid down on the bed. His expert fingers made quick work of the task. He spread her legs, and then knelt on the floor in front of her. His hands glided up her legs, then pushed them further apart, to expose her sex.

He explored her with his tongue, making her moan with pleasure. His attention was relentless, and she cried out as her orgasm hit her like a wave.

When she'd recovered, she asked him to stand up so she could undress him. She slowly revealed his body, exploring each exposed part until he was shaking. She stepped back to admire her work, causing him to groan at the loss of her touch.

This was where the Lilly got her thrills — seeing men desperate for her. She loved to make them beg for it. There was no better ego boost in the world.

"What do you want, Sam?"

"You. I want you."

"How do you want me?"

"Any way I can get you."

"Do you want me like this?" she asked as she got down on her knees in front of him. Looking up, she innocently asked, "Do you want me to suck your cock?"

"God, yes!"

"Or maybe you want me to touch it?"

"That too."

"Maybe I should just sit here and look at it for a while. What do you think?"

"Nooo. You have to touch it. I can't stand it."

"All right, I'll give you what you want," she said and caressed his throbbing member with her index finger.

"More. I need more than that."

"My, aren't we greedy?"

"Please. You're killin' me."

"Well, we can't have that. How about I give it a little lick, like a lollypop? Would that be better?"

"Oh, yeah. Do that."

She ran her tongue around the tip of his cock, then stopped and looked up at him again.

"Argh! Don't stop. That was sooo good."

"You want some more?"

"Yes, please."

This time she ran her tongue along his entire length, then quickly took the whole thing into her mouth. His startled gasp showed her how excited he was, but she wasn't finished teasing him and promptly let him slide back out of her mouth.

"What're you doing to me?" He moaned and tried to grab her head and force himself back into her mouth.

She sat back on her heels and said, "Oh, no you don't. Touching me is against the rules. You just have to stand there and be a good boy. If you're good enough, then I'll give you a reward."

"Oh, God. What do I have to do?"

"Just stand there, as still as you can, and let me look at you. I love it when you're so excited for me. Let's see, what should I give you if you're good?" She pretended to think about this for a full minute while he stood completely still. Suddenly, she got up and went to the bathroom, returning a few moments later with a glass filled with ice.

She knelt in front of him again and slowly put an ice cube into her mouth. She sucked it suggestively until it had melted, then took him into her cold mouth.

He gasped again, but remained still. She ran her cold tongue around his cock, feeling it grow stiffer as her mouth warmed up.

At this point, Sam was nearly frantic with need and she was just about to take pity on him when he pulled out of her mouth. She looked up at him, confused.

"Come here. I want you bent over this chair. I think I need to punish you for being such a tease."

She did as he asked and he was behind her in an instant. He grabbed her hips and rammed his cock deep inside her. She uttered a surprised "oomph," then held on for dear life while he pounded out the frustration she'd caused.

His forcefulness and relentless thrusts soon had her on the brink again. Just when she thought she couldn't stand anymore, her climax tore through her and sent Sam over the edge too.

When he'd got himself under control, Sam pulled out and slapped her ass — hard. "That's for being a naughty girl and teasing me," he said in a stern voice. "Now, stand up and don't turn around until I tell you."

She heard him walk way. *Did I go too far? I thought we were having fun. I know I was.*

"Okay, bad girl, you can turn around now," Sam said as he came back into the room. When she turned, Sam handed her a little blue box.

"What's this for? I thought you were mad at me." *This is just like in the movies — so romantic. I could really go for a guy like him, but he's married, married with a capital M.*

She opened the Tiffany's box and gasped. A gorgeous ring that sparkled with elegance was nestled inside.

He took the ring box from her, pulled the ring out of it and put it on her finger. "I want you to know how special you are to me."

Those are magical words, but the implied "we can never be more than this" part is a little disappointing. She admired the sapphire surrounded by diamonds and thought, *Diamonds and sapphires are definitely a girl's best friend.* "Thank you, Sam. You're special to me, too."

After a short swim in the magnificent pool, they had drinks poolside and talked. Lilly hated these contrived conversations. She'd say something, then Sam would reply. She figured neither of them was telling the truth;

it was all just a game and a bridge to their next sexual encounter.

This time, Sam surprised her. "Lilly, honey, I don't know much about you. I want to know everything there is to know. I think it's time. Don't you? You know you can trust me. "

"Of course I trust you," she said, lying. "It's just that I'm not all that interesting. I was a good student, got into medical school and paying for that put me in a financial bind. I needed more money, so I started working for Rayna. Now I can pay my bills and take care of my grandmother without stressing about money."

Lilly didn't want to talk about herself. Talking about herself meant talking about her past, which would mean she'd have to face what waited for her in those memories. *Not happening today.*

She quickly changed the subject and told Sam she wanted to shower and "make herself presentable" before dinner. She liked having Sam to herself here on this beautiful estate. *Stop right there,* she admonished. *That fantasy can't go any farther. Fuck him, have fun, no emotions involved.*

They went inside and Sam followed her into the shower. *Boy, Sam's really into it today. I can't believe he's ready to go again this soon.*

Knowing how much he wanted her really turned Lilly on. He kissed her deeply as his hands roamed her body. When his fingers found her pussy, she was already hot and wet. *Apparently Sam's not the only one ready for another round!*

This time was slower than the last and they took time to enjoy each other. She poured some of the silky perfumed body wash into her hand and then used it to soap every inch of Sam's body. When he couldn't take it anymore, he pushed her against the shower's tiled wall and lifted her onto his stiff member.

Using the wall to support her, he slowly made love to her as the warm water beat down on them both. Lilly was surprised by Sam's stamina, and enjoyed every minute of it.

This time when they found their release, it seemed like it was something more than sex, and it was difficult for Lilly to keep reminding herself that she was providing a service that Sam was paying for — nothing else.

As he slowly lowered her feet to the floor, Sam said, "Guess I got a little excited. It's our one-year anniversary, and I wanted to make it special."

"You're such a sweetie. It has been a great year and I'm glad I got to know you. How about we dry off and spend some time cuddling? You've worn me out today, stud."

"Yes, I think I could use a rest after that performance! Are you hungry?"

"A little. I think you definitely need to eat something."

"Why's that?"

"You know I'm a doctor."

Sam laughed. "So am I. What's that got to do with anything?"

"You're a diabetic. Right?"

"Yes. I didn't know you watched me that closely."

"Sam," she said, and sat down on the bed beside him, "we don't have to talk about his again if you don't want to, but I know you need to eat something. You know the symptoms as well as I do. So, let's order some room service right now."

"How long have you known?"

"I notice things like that, so it's been a while," Lilly said and handed him a bottle of orange juice from the mini bar. "Drink. Doctor's orders." When he drank it instead of arguing, she had her answer.

Lilly had never had such a beautiful weekend. Sam was perfect, but she knew it was only a matter of time before he'd have to let her go. She was sure goodbye was in their future, whether he thought so or not. *I fuck him for money. Why would he want a serious relationship with a woman who does that?* She asked herself that same question every time they were together.

Who's the Blonde?

ealty was a rude shock after the lovely weekend she'd spent with Sam. It was sort of like waking up from a wonderful dream, only to be greeted by all the demands of everyday life.

Wouldn't it be great to live in that dream world permanently? she wondered as she walked toward the table Rayna had reserved for their lunch meeting. There was a stunning blonde woman she didn't know sitting with Rayna. She looked vaguely familiar, and Lilly slowed her approach to try to figure out who she was.

Ah. She's the one who was with Ben at the Warrington Bar a few months ago. Lilly had secretly made up several stories about this diva. Seeing her with Ben had made the green-eyed monster put in an appearance — especially after the blonde kissed him. *Why the hell is that woman here? Hmm, never thought I'd meet the bitch, but here she is and I guess I'm having lunch with her.*

Lilly took a deep breath, plastered a smile on her face and projected some less than genuine friendliness. It was good that Rayna didn't know her well enough to know she was faking it.

She wanted to turn around and walk away, but Rayna was the boss and she expected these little meetings. Rayna wasn't in to idle chitchat, so Lilly knew something important was going on.

When she finally made it to the table, Rayna said in a serious tone, "Lilly, honey, I'd like you to meet Elizabeth Lawrence."

"Nice to meet you." Lilly smiled and sat down. "Sorry I'm late — one too many emergencies today."

Elizabeth seemed to understand. "You got that right. We all have those days."

Rayna seemed preoccupied and the conversation continued without her. She kept watching the door as Elizabeth took over the conversation. "Good to meet you, dear. How's everything in doctor world? I've always liked doctors. They make great pets and good fucks, plus if something bad happens you've got your own MD right there in your bed."

Lilly wasn't easily surprised, but Elizabeth's comment didn't fit with her straight-laced look. She wasn't quite sure how to respond, since she still didn't know who this woman was or why she was here.

It seemed like Rayna and Elizabeth had an agenda. Lilly made a conscious decision to keep her thoughts to herself until she found out what it was. *This is one of those times where less is more.*

Rayna made it her business to know what her escorts liked, so she'd ordered a coffee for Lilly instead of a drink. This familiarity unnerved Lilly; she was a private person didn't like it that Rayna always seemed to know everything about her life, even things she hadn't told her.

What Lilly didn't know was Rayna had assigned undercover bodyguards to each of her girls. That was how she kept tabs on them and knew so much about their lives. She wanted to keep her girls safe, and had been doing a good job of it until now.

"Why the meeting, Rayna? I know you're not a meeting person."

"We have a serious problem."

"We? What happened?" *Damn I hate being in the dark.*

"Go on, Rayna," Elizabeth chimed in. "Talk to us. It seems like Lilly's pressed for time."

"It's okay, Rayna, take your time. You seem upset."

Despite what Lilly said, Elizabeth waved Rayna on, trying to speed things up. She didn't want to be there all night.

The normally straightforward and to the point Rayna seemed rattled. "A couple of the girls had a rough go with their men the other night."

Lilly suddenly became a little uneasy. *That could've been me. I've been naïve to think nothing bad could happen on my dates. I'd better be more careful.* "Okay, you've got my full attention. Who got hurt?"

"Lilly, if I thought it'd help I'd tell you, but I'm trying to protect the girls while we investigate."

"Oh," Lilly said, stunned.

Rayna was apologetic. "You know me. I clear all the clients myself, just to be safe. I don't know how this happened."

"Come on, Rayna, I think you should tell me who it was."

"Honey, please let me find out more first."

Elizabeth gave Rayna a look and shook her head. "I love you girl, but you do realize some of your girls have their own clients. Trust me, I know that for a fact. Honesty doesn't fit into this scenario all the time. Lies come easy for us — it's part of the job."

Lilly wondered how Elizabeth could be so cold. What did she know about needing money? Her $3,000 bag and $1,000 shoes told her story loud and clear.

Lilly still wanted to know who Elizabeth Lawrence was and why the hell she was putting in her two cents about Rayna's business. *Maybe she's a cop or something, though she's too beautiful to dirty her hands working. Women like her don't usually do much other than look pretty and let their men take care of them.*

"So, let me get this straight," Lilly said. "You have a few girls who got beaten up by their dates and you're taking responsibility. Is that it or is there more?"

Elizabeth smiled at Lilly's kick ass attitude. She liked women who were confident to the point of being bitchy.

Lilly was barely five-two, probably a little too skinny and stacked. Men liked her because she was confident and not afraid to show it. That combination was also a plus in the escort world and her earnings showed it.

Elizabeth ran a critical eye over Lilly and decided all that was needed was a little tweaking to up her game. A great pair of shoes and a tight leather skirt would go a long way toward creating the image Elizabeth wanted.

Lilly was doing some evaluating of her own at the same time. Elizabeth had poise and Lilly was a little in awe of her. *No wonder Ben was with her, she's stunning.*

"Lilly, I need your help so I have to tell you a few things that none of my other escorts know," Rayna said, completely ignoring what was going on at the table.

"You know me, Rayna. My lips are sealed." Lilly regretted saying those words the second they came out of her mouth. *I don't want any trouble; I've worked too hard to lose it all now. Even though I love the money, I could give it up in a second if I need to... Couldn't I?*

Rayna knew she had to come clean. Lilly needed answers. "Okay, let's start with Elizabeth's connection to all this. She's my partner. She used to work for me and was a top earner just like you. She met Oliver Lawrence while she was on the job and ended up marrying him.

"Anyway, back then I was in debt and just one week short of closing up shop. When Elizabeth found out, she gave me a loan and we became partners and then good friends. She's the reason my business is so successful."

Elizabeth smiled at her friend and said, "No way would I ever let you go down, Rayna."

Lilly wasn't quite satisfied with that explanation. Rayna could tell, and added, "Have you ever heard of the Lawrence Business Group?"

"Of course I have. Anyone who lives in Chicago knows that name." Lilly suddenly had an "a-ha moment." *Elizabeth is the Elizabeth Lawrence, socialite and queen of the ball. Now that's big money! I wouldn't mind finding someone like that for myself. Shallow much, Lilly?*

Rayna was visibly nervous as they talked, but when Ben Charles walked in, everything changed. Elizabeth waved him over to the table. As he walked toward them, Lilly heard Elizabeth whisper, "Too bad he's got a wife. That Ben Charles is one hunk of burnin' love."

Lilly couldn't breathe as she looked at Ben standing there being his usual devilishly handsome self. If Lilly could've ripped off his clothes and fucked him right there on the table, she would have. She was glad to see him but she refused to let him know it. *A girl has her pride, especially when she's the anonymous asshole that left before saying good-bye.*

Apparently Rayna and Elizabeth know Ben pretty well. Maybe Elizabeth is his lover. As Elizabeth got up to hug him, it seemed like her body slid right into his with practiced familiarity. After greeting her, he bent to kiss Rayna's cheek and she immediately appeared to relax.

Hmm, apparently Ben's been in all of our beds. I don't like that one bit. The jealous reaction surprised her.

Elizabeth motioned for Ben to sit down and then made the introductions. "Lilly, meet Benjamin Charles."

Ben shook her hand as if he was happy to see her, but when she smiled and pretended she didn't know him, he did the same. "Nice to meet you, Lilly."

"Same here."

Lilly couldn't take her eyes off him. *I'm such a jerk. How could I have been so insensitive to such a nice guy? Married guy. Remember that. Note to self … he's married. Can't get him out of my head, though. He was just a one-night stand, but if I'd done things differently maybe it could've been so much more.*

Until that moment she had no idea how much she really wanted to be with this man again. *Damn, I'm always fantasizing about married men, first Sam and now Ben.*

Thank goodness for my one time Charlies. I probably wouldn't recognize those guys on the street if I saw them. I need to treat them all that way so I can keep my sanity!

She snapped back to reality and realized she'd been staring at Ben. *One fuck doesn't constitute a relationship, so just stop it! It was just a pick up. He probably really doesn't remember me and I'm just acting like a silly teenager. Grow up, Lilly.*

Rayna couldn't help but notice how uncomfortable Lilly became as soon as Ben walked in. She also noticed the way Ben watched every move Lilly made. *One thing I know is men, and I'm sure something's going on with those two.*

Rayna couldn't think about that right now, she had more pressing problems, like being down three girls. She had to find out why this was happening and if any of the others escorts were at risk.

She realized she was going to have to lie to everyone to keep her girls working. She didn't like doing that, but didn't think she had a choice.

Ben had reluctantly agreed to meet with Rayna and Elizabeth. It wasn't exactly what FBI investigators did, but Elizabeth had him by the balls and there was no way out of it.

He actually disliked Elizabeth but knew he had to pay for the sins committed in his youth. He'd hired an escort for himself and two of his buddies for a bachelor party gone wild. The party got too wild, and Elizabeth ended up getting them out of a mess that would've cost them their jobs.

Being the cunt she always was, she used that night to hold him hostage repeatedly. So, when she called he came running and he hated every minute of it.

This time was different. He was deeply disturbed by the cruelty of the attacks on the escorts.

Ben whispered in Elizabeth's ear. "Meet me outside."

She shook her head no but Ben whispered again. "If you want me to help, get your ass outside or I'm out of here. Obviously Rayna needs my help."

Elizabeth stood up and in her usual sultry way removed herself from the table. Naturally, several of the men in the restaurant nearly drooled as she sashayed by.

Lilly was puzzled by the whole situation. *Why show up only to turn around and leave with that woman?*

"Rayna, while they're gone, you need to tell me what happened. Were you threatened, too? Should I be worried? Not knowing is probably worse than finding out the truth."

Rayna teared up. "I check every damn person that comes through my doors but sometimes the girls take a party on their own. That's what happened this time. Some lunatic cut up their beautiful faces and shaved their heads, then knocked them unconscious. They haven't been able to tell anyone who it was.

"Since I didn't know about it, I have no idea who could be responsible. It's making me crazy not knowing. Ben Charles is the best investigator around. We hope he can figure out who did this."

"Which girls got hurt? I won't say a word, I'd just feel better knowing."

"It was Samantha, Megan and Carolyn."

Lilly's heart dropped. She knew all three of them. What was worse was that they'd asked her to join them on that fateful night, but she'd had a double shift and couldn't go.

She saw Ben and Elizabeth get into a black limo that had pulled up outside the restaurant. *Must be nice to have a limo at your beck and call.*

When Elizabeth and Ben got into the limo, she noticed the person in the driver's seat wasn't her regular driver. "Where's Max?"

"Max is on a break. If you're a good girl, he'll be back," Ben said. "Elizabeth, meet Jake. Remember him? We were the ones you brilliantly set up that night. Drugs? Don't have much of an imagination, do you?"

"It worked didn't it?"

"Yes, but every dog has its day. And, honey, this time you're the dog."

"Ben, don't be such an asshole. You know I love that little, and I do mean little, dick of yours. It's so cute and small. You remember me sucking it, don't you?"

"Cut the shit and let's get down to business. You got yourself into some hot water and we know it. Rayna was planning to retire and you were going to be more involved. Well, my dear, you *are* involved and you just might be going away to a federally sponsored hotel."

"You're threating me? Ben, you're an idiot. Why I thought you were different is beyond me. You're just like all the others."

Jake turned around. "He's not threatening you, I am. He's nicer than me. I want some names. I'll give you a few days to make your decision or I'll have you picked up and booked. Don't for a moment think I won't. If you're thinking about hurting Rayna, I wouldn't do that either. We know this is all you."

Ben flashed her a sinister smile. "You better listen, honey. He can be a real asshole when he's pissed off. Also, for anyone concerned, I'm a private investigator. For now, we're going to leave the FBI out of it."

"What if I don't come up with those names?"

Jake seemed a bit more irritable than Ben. "Listen, honey, you need to stop the bullshit. We know you're runnin' the drugs through Rayna's service. Seems like everybody but Rayna knows about it. You set those girls up and they got hurt, so let's not play Mother Theresa."

***

The next night Lilly had planned to return to The Harrington bar but she got sidetracked when Rayna called and asked her if she wanted to go see the injured girls. They weren't at Chicago Memorial. Instead, they were in Indiana at a private hospital under police protection. At this point Rayna didn't trust anyone.

The girls were understandably upset and there were a lot of tears and hugs all around. Lilly thought the injuries would heal without leaving too many visible scars, but the psychological scars would be much worse.

The visit was a short one, since the girls needed to recuperate and Rayna and Lilly had a long drive back. When Rayna dropped her off, Lilly went straight to bed. All escort services had been cancelled for the next week to give Ben time to find out who'd hurt the girls.

***

Two days later, Lilly returned to The Harrington. She went there to see if Ben might put in an appearance. She'd decided not to pretend anymore and just see where things went with him.

When she got there, Jacob the bartender handed her a note.

> Please meet me at the Peninsula Dessert Bar at
> 10. How can chocolate be wrong?
>
> Please come, Ben

Should I go to him or just forget this? He knows who I am and what I do. He's probably just looking for a free fuck. … It was nice being with him. Maybe I should just get him out of my system. Decision made, Lilly left the bar and headed out for some chocolate and Ben at the Pen.

When she walked into the lobby at the Peninsula, she stopped for a second to take in the scene. It was a lovely setting, and she quickly spotted Ben sitting at one of the tables, an assortment of goodies from the Chocolate Bar on the table in front of him. He smiled at her, and she walked over to join him.

"It looks like you started without me," she said as she sat down.

"I thought I'd add a few treats to the table so you wouldn't be able to resist coming over."

"Well, these do look tempting," Lilly said, as she picked up one of the lovely little French macaroons to nibble on.

"I hope there's more here to tempt you than just the deserts."

"Are you coming on to me, sir?"

"Yeah, I thought that was pretty obvious," he said and chuckled.

"Why don't you see if you can find someone to put all these treats into a box for us so we can enjoy them together later?"

"I'll get right on that," he said and signaled their server.

Minutes later they were in Ben's plush suite at the hotel. He'd already set the mood with soft music playing in the background, and the sumptuous bed turned down. As soon as the door closed, Ben pulled her so close to him she could feel his heartbeat. *This is such a foolish thing you're doing, you idiot. You can't have feelings for him. Hell, you don't even know why he's bothering with you, other than maybe he likes sex with a professional.*

Even though she knew she shouldn't, she slowly inhaled the scent of his aftershave and the underlying aroma that was purely Ben. His smell was sexy and masculine and it just made her want him that much more.

The sexual tension between them was fierce. Suddenly, he yanked up her dress and ripped off her panties. Her hands were just as busy, fingers fumbling with urgency as she tried to unzip his pants.

He brushed her hands aside and quickly removed the obstacle to their union. Their coupling was fast and hard.

Her orgasm hit like a tsunami, carrying her away on a wave of sensation. As she came down from that high, she watched Ben as his climax built. The sight was such a turn-on; she could feel a second wave building. As Ben shouted his release, she followed him, tumbling into that sexual ether.

After a few seconds, they looked at each other and laughed a bit nervously.

"So, are you going to leave like you did last time or are we going to have breakfast together this time? The blueberry pancakes you ordered for me were great."

"Of course we'll have breakfast together, but I think maybe we could do some other things together before then."

Ben was delighted that Lilly had decided to stay but their time was cut short when his cellphone rang.

When she saw his face as he listened to the call, Lilly knew their time together was about to end.

"I guess you're leaving," she said as he ended the call.

"Yeah, I have to, but you're coming with me. I'm not leaving you by yourself again until I figure out what's going on. That was Elizabeth. She wanted me to know that Rayna's been shot. She's in intensive care, and Elizabeth is staying with her until we can get there."

Lilly was happy to hear Rayna wasn't alone, but she wasn't too excited to see Elizabeth again. *That woman just rubs me the wrong way.*

They quickly got cleaned up and dressed and headed to the hospital. The ride over was tense, with each of them lost in their own thoughts.

When they got to Chicago Memorial, Lilly and Ben ended up going their separate ways. Before they even got to the nurse's station, Lilly's pager went off. She was needed in the ER and there wasn't a damn thing Ben could do to stop her from leaving. The only thing that stopped him from bodily restraining her was the man he had stationed as a male nurse, who'd be working right beside her in the ER. *No fucking way will I let anything happen to her.*

After Lilly rushed off, Ben went on to Rayna's room so he could check on her and find out what happened. When he got there, Rayna was sedated, and Elizabeth was waiting for him like a black widow in her web.

"Hey, handsome," she said seductively.

"We need to talk," he said tersely.

"Well, I don't think we should do that here. Why don't we meet tomorrow."

"Fine," he said, then turned and quickly left the room.

She's a Bitch, Girl,
and She's Gone Too Far...

Elizabeth was waiting for Jake when he got to her office, but apparently didn't have just business on her mind. She was sitting on top of her desk, wearing red lace panties and a matching bra.

"I guess all the money I give you isn't enough for a binding contract. You blind-sided me the other night and I want to know why? Do you really think I know what happened to those girls?"

"I sure the fuck do!"

"But threatening me? Really?"

"You know me, I had to go along with Ben. He's a powerful guy and I can't lose my job. You know that," Jake lied smoothly. He loved having the upper hand.

"You could lose the job. I'd give you more money — I've got plenty of that. And don't say it's because you didn't want to ask. You've never been shy about asking for more," she said and spread her legs suggestively.

"Elizabeth, are you mad? There's no time for this. Do you always think about sex?"

"Yes, and there's always time for a good fuck. I think better with a stiff dick inside me. "

"Rayna's fighting for her life and all you can think about is a good fuck? Are you that cold blooded?"

She motioned for him to come closer and stand between her legs, but he stood his ground. "Maybe my blood's a little cold but it works for me. Haven't had any complaints."

Jake regretted their brief affair for the millionth time. She always held it over his head, especially since he'd come back to her when he'd needed some extra cash. She paid well, but she was a nightmare — she had her claws in him and he was afraid she'd never let go.

She's being especially disgusting tonight. God, I wish I didn't need her help, then I could just turn around and leave. She knows everything that goes on in Chicago though, and she's probably the only one who can help me.

When she realized he wasn't moving, she got up and sashayed toward him. Her voice was soft and seductive, "I'm waiting for you, baby..."

Men were usually like putty in her hands, especially when they needed something from her. She had him by the balls and he'd have to fuck her, or she'd never talk.

"I've missed you, Jake. It's been so long. When I saw you behind the wheel of my limo, I knew I had to be with you again."

"Not now, Elizabeth. This isn't right on so many levels."

She moved closer to him; so close their bodies were touching. "We used to be on the same page."

"Not anymore."

She caressed his dick through his pants, and felt it twitch to life. Taking this as a sign, she started to unbutton his pants, but he grabbed her hands and stopped her.

"You help me and then maybe I'll help you," she said as she unbuttoned his shirt. She licked his nipple and then with slow, easy hands she slid down to unfasten his belt.

Jake knew he was lost. There was no resisting Elizabeth Lawrence. Giving in to his baser instincts, he pushed her down on the couch. "You wanna fuck? Well, better hold on to something, baby, 'cause I'm gonna pound hard and fast," he said angrily.

Rather than scaring her, his rage just made her that much wetter. *There's just something so hot about forcing a man to fuck when he really doesn't want to.*

"Get on your hands and knees like the whore you are," he ordered. "I can't stand to look at you."

She complied, and he immediately slammed into her. He hammered out all his frustration and fury, driving into her relentlessly. All he could think about was how much he hated her and how helpless he felt because he couldn't get away from her.

Elizabeth was oblivious to everything but the sensation of Jake pounding her pussy. She liked it rough, and he'd reacted exactly the way she wanted.

As Jake's fury finally wore itself out, he thrust faster and faster, trying to find release. Without the anger driving him, it was difficult to finish the deed, but he knew he had to or Elizabeth would keep him prisoner until he satisfied her.

Finally, he felt her tensing. *About time she came. Probably held back just to torture me.* As soon as he felt her tip over the edge into her climax, he drove himself to come. As soon as he'd finished, he pulled out and grabbed Elizabeth's panties to wipe himself off.

Before Elizabeth realized what he was doing, he had his pants back on and was working on buttoning his shirt. "What haven't you told me about the situation with those girls?" He knew he had to ask his questions now, while Elizabeth was still in an orgasmic haze.

"Jake, you never disappoint. It's business as usual. Before we talk business, let's talk about your wife."

"Leave Suzanna out of this. She's no longer in the picture. She was never in the picture."

"Okay, if it wasn't her, then why'd you stop coming around. I need to know."

"Fine, I'll tell you, but this is never happening again."

"If you say so, honey. "

"There are days when Suzanna just lays in bed without saying a word. She stares at the ceiling for hours at a time. Alzheimer's never gets better, only worse. I'm really not sure if she even knows who I am."

"I'm sorry. Why didn't you ever say anything?"

"Because I loved her too much. I didn't want to admit it. It would have felt like I was giving up."

Elizabeth didn't say another word she just let Jake finish getting dressed. Even she had her limits. "Okay, I'll tell you what I know about the girls…"

Unfinished Business …
Business As Usual

"The best way of keeping a secret
is to pretend there isn't one."
— Margaret Atwood, The Blind Assassin

Ben Charles agreed to meet Elizabeth at the Four Seasons Chicago Hotel, even though he didn't want to. Now, to top it off, he was running late. When he finally got to her room, she was there waiting for him, alone and barely dressed. I should've known better. She told me this was an urgent meeting. Ha! She promised to help find Rayna's shooter and help me figure out who attacked three of her escorts. She knew I wouldn't come otherwise.

Elizabeth didn't have friends; she had adversaries. Everything was a competition for her. She knew what Ben thought of her, but she also knew he couldn't seem to resist her. Guess bad habits are hard to break, and I'm the baddest of them all.

She was sitting on the bed and had dressed for the evening she had in mind —red lace panties, lots of jewelry, and nothing else. She knew her breasts were full and tempting, and knew how attractive she was to the opposite sex.

Even though he loathed the woman, Ben wanted to jump her and forget what a bitch she was. There's too much at stake. I need to keep it in my pants.

"Give me a kiss, baby," she whispered as he came closer.

"Not today, baby," he said sarcastically. "Put your clothes on. We need to talk. "

"Come on. You know I can't concentrate when I'm horny. That's why you're here. I've got an itch only you can scratch. I can see your dick twitching in your pants. I know you want me."

He just stood there, letting her beg. I'm not giving in this time.

"Come on. Just one last time for old time's sake?" she asked in her sexiest voice. "Come to mama. You don't even have to give me a present when we're done."

She must really be hard up. She always wants something in return, Ben thought. She usually wants the baubles more than the sex. He knew she still set up "appointments" for herself because she enjoyed the game and its rewards.

Ben looked at her with disgust. The groveling mess in front of him was a big turnoff; nothing like the sexy woman he first met in one of Chicago's older landmark hotels.

Back then, her blond hair was parted to frame her beautiful face and her bangs were wispy, almost covering her eyes. She had a great smile and an incredible body. She had worn a black dress that clung to breasts and accentuated her tiny waist. Her silky-smooth ivory shoulders had beckoned to him, and her gorgeous legs encased in black suede boots nearly made him tremble. She even smelled good — like dark chocolate and cherries.

She'd shocked him when she'd said, "I'd like to be having an organism as soon as possible. How about you?" Five minutes later they were in the elevator on their way up to her room and some of the best sex he'd ever had.

Now, as he stood there looking at her hating her as much as he wanted her, he wondered what had happened to that girl. "Okay, Elizabeth, tell me why I'm here."

"You're here because you've been trying like hell to figure out what my part in Rayna's shooting was. You think I'm a suspect?"

"Yeah. Am I right?"

"You might be."

"Come on, Elizabeth, let's not play games. I can see right through you."

"I agree, no games," she said as she walked over to her bag and pulled out a .45.

"Elizabeth, what the hell are you doing? Put that fucking gun away."

Elizabeth turned and fired three shots into his chest. She didn't even flinch as she watched him fall back against the door. She grinned and said, "Sorry about that, baby."

She quickly threw on her robe just as three big goons entered the room. "Clean up this mess and get it out of here."

She sashayed toward the bathroom, slipped off her robe and turned on the shower. When it was warm, she got in and casually washed away the evidence. Shooting a former lover was business as usual for her.

Moving On Up and Loving It

There was no doubt about it — Elizabeth Lawrence was one cold bitch, and a rich one too. She'd seen to it that Rayna was one step closer to the grave, and had taken control of her business. Her doting husband wasn't a well man either, so she'd soon have complete control of his money as well. She knew the time was right to make her move. *I'm moving on up and loving it. I've got plans and no one is going to get in my way.*

If she'd been born rich maybe she'd have a less aggressive approach to life, but the thought of losing it all after working so hard to get it was her worst nightmare. Avoiding that possibility is what drove her. She had to be sure that never happened to her.

Every morning she went for a run in the park on Lake Shore Drive. No matter how harsh the weather, she was always there. This morning she was thinking about her life, the people in it, and what she could never have again. Thinking about the past was never a good thing for her.

There he is, the love of my life, just sitting on a park bench waiting for me, she thought. *That can't be right. He's dead. I mourned him. Why is he here?* She kept running as he called out to her, "Lizzie, it's me. Stop for a minute. Please, baby. I need to talk to you."

"William Carter, is that you?"

"It's me, honey. I'm here for you. Come sit with me. Please?"

She pinched herself. "I must be dreaming. You can't be here — you're dead. "

"I'm really here. I had to come. You're on such a destructive path and I need to stop you. Why do you do these things? Do you wanna end up dead?"

"Yeah, I've wanted that for a long time. When you and Janna were killed in that car accident, I didn't go outside for six months. I kept the drapes drawn and the shades pulled down. I didn't want to see the sun; I wanted to die."

"You had your whole life ahead of you. Why would you waste it?"

"I knew my life could never be good without you and Janna."

"Time passed and you're a different person now."

Elizabeth felt a few tears trickle down her face. "I've been with lots of men, but none of them were you. I don't like to be alone. When I'm alone, I think about how horrible my life is. I've got money now — lots of it. I'm a Chicago socialite of all things, and people know me. I'd trade it all to have you and Janna back. Why are you here now, after all this time? "

"You need me because you have to make some changes. Lizzie, you were the most wonderful wife and mother. Where'd that loving person go?"

"I know I'm a mean bitch now, and that's the way it's going stay. I have to protect myself. I can't get close to anyone and go through that kind of loss again."

William took her hand and said, "I love you and I want you to be happy. Let go of us. You know we can't come back."

"I don't want to let go!"

William shook his head and started to walk away.

"Billy, honey, kiss me one last time," she pleaded. "Please?"

He put his arms around her and held her tightly as she cried. She closed her eyes and felt his lips touch hers like a whisper. It was a wonderful balm for her tired soul, and she felt transformed by it. When she opened her eyes, he was gone. There she stood as always, alone. After she'd recovered from the ghostly encounter, she continued her run.

Because Guilty Pleasures had a reputation to maintain, the attack on Rayna had been kept out of the media as much as possible. The business was quite lucrative so there was plenty of money to keep the wheels greased and the press silent.

Elizabeth decided to have Rayna transferred to Lilly's hospital so she could start implementing her plan. Rayna was still unresponsive, and there didn't seem to be much hope. Even if she woke up, she probably wouldn't be the same person she'd been before the shooting.

After days of waiting for some improvement in Rayna's condition, Elizabeth summoned Lilly for yet another meeting — she was working hard at the "wear her down" part of the plan. Lilly had already sat through quite a few of these heart to heart talks and Elizabeth could tell she was getting tired of the bullshit. *I know she wants to tell me to go to hell but she can't because she's not ready to leave Guilty Pleasures.* So, Lilly would be joining Elizabeth for dinner because she had no choice and that was that. Second thoughts didn't matter.

Lilly

Because Lilly actually had time to dress for dinner, she decided to look stylish for a change. The more depressed she got, the more she worried about her looks. It bothered her that sometimes she looked in the mirror and saw her mother staring back. *Have I become my*

*mother? Am I a depressed woman on the verge of crisis? …
No, not yet. Still fighting.*

She put on her favorite black leather dress — the tight one that showed off her perfect figure. Then, she added her new expensive short black boots with the fringe. For the finishing touch, she put on the diamond broach Jonah Michaels, her favorite client, had given her. *Jonah was a good man,* she thought as she pinned on his gift. *He was always on my side. The money he left me was a surprise, but the conditions attached to it are impossible, actually there was only one. I had to quit working as an escort immediately. Can't seem to give it up. Damn I'm screwed up.*

She was meeting Elizabeth at a small suburban Italian restaurant where they could have some privacy as they talked. When she arrived, Elizabeth was already seated and waiting for her. She looked impatient.

"Look at you, Dr. Peters. You clean up pretty damn good," Elizabeth said in a slightly mocking tone.

Lilly put on her fake smile and said, "So, why am I here? You know I don't have much free time."

"I don't care about your schedule," Elizabeth answered in her cool insensitive manner. "I asked you here because you need to know a few things."

"Such as?" she asked sarcastically; she couldn't seem to help that tone when it came to Elizabeth.

"Can we call a truce for the evening? I need you to promise that what I'm about to tell you will remain confidential."

"Who the hell would I tell? Believe me, I can just walk away as easy as one two three. I've done it before. So if you don't trust me, I'll leave right now," she said as she stood up.

"I know that. There's not a whole lot about you that I don't know. My investigators were thorough. Climb down off your high horse and sit your ass down."

"You need to stop screwing with me. Just say what you came to say so I can leave."

Elizabeth grabbed hold of her wrist and said plaintively, "I'm going to need your help. I want to find out why Rayna was shot. I think you want to know the same thing. So, stop acting like a child and help me."

Because what Elizabeth had to say involved Rayna, Lilly decided to stay and listen. At first they were both angry but after a couple of drinks they had calmed down and the conversation was almost civil.

"How well do you think you know Rayna?" Elizabeth asked.

"Pretty well, I suppose." Lilly didn't want to let Elizabeth know she wasn't close to Rayna; she'd just used her because she was a good listener. She still didn't trust Elizabeth.

"You do know, my dear, your friend Rayna was a drug dealer."

Don't call me "dear," bitch. And while you're at it, don't fuckin' lie to me either. No way was Rayna a drug dealer. "Elizabeth, you can't be serious. Rayna was a nurse for the better part of her life. She helped people. Do you really expect me to believe that drug dealer bullshit?"

"I guess you didn't know her as well as you thought."

"Why don't you just tell me what's going on. I'm not stupid and neither are you. Let's move past the bullshit portion of the evening and get down to facts."

Elizabeth wasn't planning on giving Lilly much information but realized she'd have to change her strategy if she wanted Lilly's help. "This whole situation is becoming dangerous. I need you to be patient and keep working for me like nothing's happened. We have clients expecting service and you're the one I'd like to send to them. You're the best there is, besides me of course."

"So, business as usual?"

"Precisely."

"That can't happen. You should know better than to ask me to play stupid. It's not safe out there."

"Of course it's safe. I have so many guys out there watching you and the others, there's no way anything else can happen."

"I don't need bodyguards. This life was wrong for me from the start. I'm a doctor. That's always been my dream. I think it's time for me to get out of the business."

"I don't think that's going to happen any time soon. You owe us quite a bit of money. You should've thought about that before you bought one of the most expensive condos in Chicago. I think you like the money just as much as I do. You'll never be able to quit."

"I can walk away any time."

"Really? Maybe you should think about what it'll be like having to scrape by, barely being able to pay your bills like in the old days. Look at you, dressed in clothes that cost as much as some people make in a month. I can't see you going back to shopping at Becky's Bargains."

"I really don't care what you think."

"Maybe, but you owe me money. If you're serious about walking away from the business, pay up and get your little ass on out of here. No strings. But if you try to stiff me, I *will* find you. The company's international, you know, so I have a wide reach."

"It is *not* international."

"You're looking at the biggest investor in Guilty Pleasures. I know everything about this business. Did you really think this was a mom and pop business? Honey, we're worldwide."

Lilly was speechless.

Elizabeth laughed. "Are you that naïve? You might as well face it. Rayna, for all practical purposes, is gone. Even if she wakes up, she won't be the same. You're gonna have to deal with me."

"You seem have all the answers. How do I know you're not lying?"

"Why don't you ask Ben Charles? He's the one who knows everything about everyone. Did you think he just *happened* to be at the bar that night you met? Believe me, sweetie, nothing that happened to you in the last year was by accident."

"Ben? Why ask Ben?"

"Just for the record, Rayna fucked Ben long before you or I did. She almost married him. Bet you didn't know that. She could get men to do anything. I learned everything I know from her."

Lilly was horrified. *Three girls have been attacked and severely injured and Rayna's on life support and all she can do is lie to me?*

Elizabeth took one last sip of her Martini and said, "Why don't we leave this discussion until later? I'll let you think about what I've said and we can talk more tomorrow."

"You're kidding me, right? You drop this bombshell on me and then you wanna leave? I need answers, and I need them now."

"That's all I have for you for now. I can tell you're angry, so I think we should wait until later to talk more. You need to calm down and think about your reality."

"You need to give me more."

"Okay, you're not going to be happy when you hear this. Rayna was part of a deal that went sideways and that's why we're in this fuckin' mess. Your idol was a drug dealer, plain and simple."

I can't believe this is true. I did not sign up for this.

When Bad Things Happen, Hide

Rayna Rogers died later that evening, and Lilly felt lost. She needed a drink and headed to the bar in at the Harrington Hotel. *Losing Rayna is harder than I thought. I didn't think I cared that much. Now it's too late to tell her... she's gone. She was the only one I could really talk to about my life and I really need someone to talk to today. I think I'm going to get a drink, and keep drinking until I don't feel anything anymore.*

As she headed to her favorite hangout, she hoped her bartender friend, Jacob, would be working, but he wasn't behind the bar. Jacob had a great smile and she found him deliciously appealing. He was younger than her and African-American, which reminded her of her husband and all the hurt that went along with that story. That's why she'd never pursued him.

Great, just another disappointment to add to this suck-ass day! First, I get divorce papers delivered to me at work, then Rayna dies and now I can't even enjoy the Jacob eye candy. I think that calls for vodka, and lots of it.

She ordered vodka on the rocks from Maxwell, another of the hotel's regular bartenders, and told him to keep them coming.

God ... divorce papers. I can't believe Cooper finally agreed to let me go. Just wish he hadn't decided to send the papers to work. No one knows I'm married. Hopefully no one will be curious about why a courier was tracking me down today.

Cooper's an asshole, but this whole mess isn't completely his fault. His snobby family can claim that distinction. They made my life a living hell and he wouldn't do anything about it. Can anybody blame me for leaving? I finally just couldn't take it anymore. It's too bad, really, because I did *love him.*

After another vodka, she wasn't ruling out going home with someone from the bar. It probably wasn't in her best interest but sometimes when she was feeling down she surprised herself with a new low.

Suddenly, Jacob came walking over to her in all his sexy glory. *He looks so good in that tight t-shirt.* She fanned herself. *He needs to be kissed hard in all the right places, and I might be just the one to do it. What the hell?*

It's been a bad day and I need something to take my mind off my troubles.

"Looks like you're serious tonight, Doc. Vodka on the rocks? Why are you hittin' the hard stuff?"

"You heard about Rayna?"

"I did, from Elizabeth. I just met with her. Man, she's a bitch. Being an escort suddenly isn't as appealing as it used to be."

"You got that right, honey." *Woops! I called him honey.*

"Are you staying in or quitting? With Rayna gone, I'm afraid there's gonna be a lot of changes — and not good ones."

Lilly nodded yes, but she didn't mean it. *As soon as I get the cash together to pay my loan, I'm out of the business. No need to tip my hand just yet though.*

"I get the feeling that bitch is gonna be trouble for all of us," Jacob added.

"You can say that again. Pretty soon she'll be the widow of a very rich man, which will only make things worse because she'll have even more money and power. Her husband is barely hanging on, you know, but you don't see her crying about it. Elizabeth isn't just mean; she's a selfish bitch.

Jacob was a little surprised by the venom in Lilly's voice. He'd never heard her say anything like that before. *The liquor must've loosened her tongue. Wonder what else is gettin' loose... If she'd let down her defenses, I'd love to kiss those soft lips and then take her to my place, ease off that lacy bra and kiss every part of her body.* He smiled, enjoying every moment of his little fantasy.

"Jacob? Jacob, where'd you go? You were a million miles away. What are you smilin' about?"

"What?"

"Thinkin' about the girl of your dreams?"

"Yep. The girl of my dreams."

"So, you're back with your girlfriend?"

"Nope, that train has left the station. She's not comin' back and I'm good with that. Just took me some time to regroup."

Lilly didn't say anything. She was thinking about sunning on a chez lounge on a sandy beach, sitting with her favorite new man, Jacob. *That's a surprising thought. Hmmm…*

Lilly had heard chitchat at the hospital about Jacob's prowess as a lover. Apparently he knew how to romance a woman and make love like there was no tomorrow. *No wonder he's at the top of the list with the female clients!*

Lilly asked Jacob for a refill, but when he came back he was carrying cup of coffee instead. "You're a lightweight and I think you've had enough of the hard stuff for one night."

"I won't tell if you don't." Lilly knew she'd had too much to drink. In fact, she wondered if she could even walk without tripping.

She waved goodbye to Max, he'd been nice to her all evening. "Hey, Jacob, Max is kind of cute. What do you know about him?"

"He's happily married, Doc. Don't get any sexy ideas about him," Jacob said, feeling surprisingly jealous.

"Aren't they *all* happily married?" *I like it when he calls me Doc.*

"Just so you know, he doesn't work for Rayna and he doesn't know we're escorts."

"That's too bad. Looks like he might be good in bed."

"I think it's time for you to go home. Let me get you a taxi."

"Don't want to go home. Too lonely. Maybe I'll call for an Uber. Sometimes the drivers are kind of cute."

"Nope. I'll take you home," Jacob said quickly. "Max, can you cover for me?"

"Sure, Jacob, no problem."

Jacob helped Lilly stand and said, "You've had too much to drink and I don't think you should be in anyone's bed tonight."

"How about *your* bed? I've heard you're pretty damn good. Maybe we should give it a try." She smiled thinking she might get to see if the gossip was true. Then, she passed out.

Jacob caught her as she folded, scooped her up in his arms and quickly got her out of the bar. This wasn't exactly how he'd imagined it in his dreams. *She's light as a feather,* he thought. *Too bad she's drunk. Wonder if she'll remember what she just said. Doubt it! I'm not her type. Not enough zeros in the bank.*

Lilly woke up in her bed, alone. She was dressed in sweats and a t-shirt. *Damn, we had sex and I don't remember it! Must've changed into these clothes after.* She quickly got up only to be caught off guard when she heard someone in her apartment.

As she peeked down the hall, she saw Jacob who seemed to feel quite comfortable in her kitchen. He was making blueberry pancakes. The smell was heavenly. *How the hell did he know that blueberry pancakes are my favorite comfort food? OMG if we didn't fuck, did we talk? I'm not drinking anymore. Oh, God, what did I tell him?*

Jacob had the music turned up and he was singing so loudly that he didn't hear her in the hall. She ran into the bathroom and looked at herself in the mirror. *Damn, I look like shit!* Her hair was frizzy and her makeup smeared. She washed her face while she tried to piece together what had happened with Jacob.

I just want to hide until I get things figured out. She'd had that reaction whenever something bad happened ever since her mother's funeral. She'd been too young to understand why her mother killed herself, so she just hid away from the world. *That was the beginning of my downward spiral. I don't think I've ever come out of it.*

God, what made me go there? *Hell, it's just Jacob. He already knows a lot of my secrets and he hasn't told anyone. I think I'm paranoid now, on top of all my other issues. Maybe I need to see a professional. They wouldn't be able to tell anyone what I said and I could get it off my chest. … Hmm, that's an idea. I'm going to find a psychiatrist and unload all this crap I've been carrying around for all these years. Surely I'll feel better after that.*

Rayna, You Fooled Us All

The funeral for Rayna Rogers was a virtual who's who of Chicago. There were lawyers, doctors, corporate executives, restaurant giants, hospital administrators and politicians and they were all there to pay their respects. Even the mayor was there. Everyone loved her and those who didn't know her were sorry they wouldn't get the chance.

Lilly couldn't believe her eyes as the parade of Chicago royalty continued. *Could this woman everyone seemed to love — a woman I liked and trusted — really be a drug dealer? Rayna, my friend, you fooled us all.*

Several weeks after Rayna's funeral, Lilly decided she was finished as an escort. The business had become too scary and no one seemed to know why Rayna was murdered. Rayna's case was still under investigation, but it was getting nowhere. There were too many high profile people involved, so it would probably end up an unsolved crime. On top of all that, she didn't trust Elizabeth.

The situation was wearing on Lilly. She couldn't sleep and didn't eat much. She was even beginning to wonder if she was a danger to her patients because she was so tired and distracted. To add to her problems, her bank account was dwindling without the extra cash from her escort activities.

Jacob seemed happy to see her when she showed up near closing time at the Harrington. She'd had another rough night at the hospital and didn't want to be alone. Double shifts were brutal, and tonight she'd had three extremely ill babies, one suicide attempt and three teen car crash victims to contend with.

"Doc, it's good to see you. Where you been hiding?" Jacob was already pouring her a drink when she reached over and stopped him.

"Just coffee tonight."

Jacob knew that things weren't going well if she didn't want her usual. "Can I help?"

She leaned over and whispered in his ear. "Have you been threatened?"

"No. Have you?"

"No. I was just checking."

Jacob didn't know her well but he could tell from the faraway look in her eyes there was more to be said. "Really?"

"Yeah. I'm just tired."

"Well if you change your mind about talking to me, I'm a pretty good listener. I *am* a bartender after all."

"I'll remember that. "

Jacob got the message and left to mix a drink for another patron at the bar. He wanted to take her in his arms and tell her everything was going to be okay, but he wasn't sure it was. Since Rayna's death, Guilty Pleasures just wasn't the same. Most of the escorts were scared and a lot of them were on the verge of quitting. He knew this because most of the escorts started their dates at the Harrington, and they all talked to him.

"Jacob, honey, you got any whipped cream?"

"Not back here but I can send Max to the kitchen. You got a sweet tooth tonight?"

"Yeah, but I don't really want whipped cream. I was just thinking about all the naughty things I could do with it and I thought maybe you'd like to join me for some fun."

"I'm not sure if that's such a good idea. You know we're not supposed to be seen together. No socializing outside of a planned event or meeting. Remember?"

"You don't look like the kind of guy who follows rules."

Jacob eye's brightened. He thought she was kidding so he relaxed and poured a shot of whiskey, then gulped it down like water.

Lilly laughed. "I've never seen you drink while you're working. Am I too much for you to handle?"

"Not at all." He laughed and gently moved her bangs out of her eyes.

"So, now that we've got that straightened out, bring on the whipped cream. I love it when men lick it off my body."

"Okay, that's maybe TMI. But, good to know."

"Aren't you just about ready to pack it in? It's late and I don't want to be alone tonight."

"Yeah, my shift's over in 10 minutes." *Damn,* he thought, *that's an invitation if I ever heard one.* He quickly motioned for one of the bar backs, "Go to the kitchen and get some whipped cream to go for this lovely lady."

"Know where we could get a room? I wanna know if what they say about you is true."

"You're kidding, right? We're in a hotel."

"You got that right," Lilly said, as she threw down her hotel keycard. "I'm the one with the room."

Jacob was a little taken aback but that didn't stop him from walking out from behind the bar to take her hand and the key. "You got me for the night!"

"Just leave some jewelry on the bed," she mumbled, and laughed.

Jacob didn't know what she meant but he didn't really care. *I'm finally gonna have her. I'll give her a night she won't forget.*

The keycard let them into a deluxe luxury suite. As soon as the door shut, Lilly grabbed him and devoured his mouth. They were a frenzy of lips, tongues and hands. She hooked one leg around his waist as they leaned against the door, and he ran his hand up and up until he discovered she was bare beneath her skirt. That pleasant surprise cranked things up a notch for Jacob, and he quickly unzipped her skirt and let it fall to the floor.

Unable to wait any longer, he lifted her into his arms and walked toward the bed, then set her down gently. She willingly unbuttoned her blouse, exposing her nearly perfect breasts for his enjoyment and then flopped back onto the bed. He opened the take-out box of whipped cream and dipped a finger into it. "I think maybe I need to put some frosting on those lovely cupcakes of yours," he said with a naughty grin.

"Oh, I think so too," Lilly said. "Cupcakes aren't good without frosting."

He dotted her nipples with cream, then stood back to admire his work. "I think they need a little more, don't you?"

Lilly moaned. "Quit teasing me, Jacob."

He climbed up her body, stopping to lick a bit of cream from each breast. "Is that better?"

"Yes. More, please!"

Jacob obliged, then said, "Your body is more beautiful than I imagined."

"You imagined me naked?"

"Yeah, pretty much since the first time I met you."

"Hmm. Well, I hope I don't disappoint you."

"I don't think that's possible," he said as he trailed kisses from her breasts down her flat stomach to her happy place. He stopped and looked up at her face. Her eyes were closed and her face was flushed.

"Why'd you stop? You were almost there!"

"Well, I think maybe I have too many clothes on to finish this job properly."

"Oh," Lilly said, her interest piqued. "Take it off, big boy. Take it all off."

Jacob gave her a sexy little impromptu striptease as he peeled off his clothes. He took his time, building her anticipation.

"Come on, what's taking so long. Let's get to the good part!"

His powerful well-muscled body moved with grace as he added a few dance moves for her benefit. Suddenly she was reminded of her ex-husband Cooper and all their fun lovemaking sessions. *God, why am I thinking about that now? I've got this beautiful, sexy man ready to rock my world and I'm stuck in the past. Come on, Lilly, snap out of it!*

Jacob had finished his performance and seemed to be waiting for a reaction. Lilly clapped and whistled. "If I had panties, I'd be throwing them about now," she said and laughed. "Now get back over here and get down to business."

He seemed to know exactly what she needed. Soon she reached the pinnacle and tumbled over, grabbing his hair and pulling him to her as she fell. When she finally released him, Jacob climbed up on the bed beside her and wrapped her in his arms.

A few minutes later, when she could function again, she said, "Wow, Jacob. The gossip about you isn't right at all. You're way better at this than anyone said!"

She turned over and ran a finger through the whipped cream, then said, "I think it's your turn to be dessert. Now, where should I put this luscious cream? Maybe here?" she asked and touched it to his nose. "No, not there," she said and kissed away the cream.

"How about here?" she asked as she touched it to one nipple and then the other. "Not there, either," she said, licking each in turn.

She giggled as he gasped, then scooped up more whipped cream and said, "I know where I'll put it," and stroked it down his rather large, erect member. "Yep, that's where it belongs. Now, should I lick this off, too?"

"Oh, please. Do it. You're killin' me, Lilly!"

She slowly ran the tip of her tongue through the cream, barely touching his skin. "Mmm, I think that's the best whipped cream I've ever tasted — so sticky and sweet. I just have to have another taste." She licked up the line of cream and then took him into her mouth.

Jacob groaned as he struggled to keep his composure. He was enjoying this game.

When she could tell Jacob was almost there, she stopped. "I think all the whipped cream is gone and I can think of a much better use for this," she said, stroking his dick.

"Oh, I can too," Jacob said, and flipped her so he was on top. He was inside her before she even realized what had happened.

Their coupling was fast and furious with both of them reaching their climax quickly. The buildup had been too good for it to last long. Panting and laughing, they lay side by side, catching their breath. Lilly pulled the sheet up over them and curled up next to Jacob.

When she was sure he was asleep, she got up and went into the bathroom. She slumped to the floor and began to cry. For some reason, she couldn't stop. *What's wrong with me?*

Jacob knocked on the bathroom door a few minutes later. *Shit! Apparently he isn't like other guys. Most men would've been asleep for at least an hour.*

"Lilly are you okay?"

"I'm fine. Just going to take a shower. Give me a few," she said as she tried to regain her composure. *Come on, Lilly, get your shit together.*

Suddenly the door opened and Jacob stood there looking handsome and sweet. He came in and sat beside her on the floor. "Why are you crying? I don't usually have this effect on women. Did I do something wrong?

"No. It's not you. You did everything right; you're perfect. It's me."

He didn't say another word, just held her while she cried.

"I'm sorry. I'm a mess. This was a mistake."

"Not for me." Jacob held her tight until she fell asleep.

Web of Deception

When the whole escort thing started, Lilly had no idea she'd end up involving herself in such an all-encompassing web of deception. Sometimes her life seemed more like the plot for a movie than real life.

It had all seemed so easy in the beginning. She'd signed up to be an escort and that was it. She needed money and being an escort got it for her. It was easy to become addicted to the life — she loved the gifts and the men who gave them to her. She knew she shouldn't let emotions enter the picture, but no matter how hard she tried she just couldn't help caring for some of her clients.

It's over now, so there's no use obsessing about it, Lilly thought.

She knew her clients missed her, and Elizabeth had made several visits to the ER trying to talk her into coming back. She'd even offered more money, which was tempting but Lilly stood firm in her decision ... for now anyway. She really didn't want to work with Elizabeth or be associated with her in any way, however she wasn't sure if she could stay away. *Maybe Elizabeth was right. I might be cut from the same cloth as her. What a dreadful thought.*

Several weeks later, her condo and expensive lifestyle were quickly eating up her savings. She realized she might have to bite the bullet and go back to being an escort. When Elizabeth's phone number came up on her phone for the millionth time, she decided to answer. It was time.

"Lilly, before you say anything, I really need to talk to you. I'm not taking no for an answer. Stay right where you are. I'll come to you. "

Several minutes later, Elizabeth came into the waiting room where Lilly was sitting and said, "About time you decided to talk to me."

"I can only spare a couple of minutes. I have patients who need me."

Elizabeth gave her an irritated look. "Let's just face reality. I haven't got time to smooth your ruffled feathers. We need to talk and lay our cards on the table. Let's go to the coffee shop downstairs."

"Can't we talk here? We're short staffed and I really can't leave. Just tell me what you came here to say."

"You know my husband has a seat on this hospital's board and during his illness he gave me the proxy. That means I'm in charge of the new hires *and* who stays and who goes. You better start playing nice with me, or you might be the next to go. Since I have your fate in my hands, I think you can spare a few minutes to talk to me in the location I choose. We're going downstairs for some coffee."

Lilly glared at her.

"You know you're not going to win this battle, so you might as well just submit."

"Whatever," Lilly said grudgingly.

"You know about the new children's wing, don't you?"

Lilly nodded, waiting for the other shoe to drop.

"Can you guess who paid for that wing?"

"No, but I'm sure you're going to tell me."

"The Elizabeth and Oliver Lawrence Kid's Foundation. So, don't forget who's running this show, 'cause it's certainly *not* you."

Lilly took a deep breath and watched Elizabeth revel in her newly obtained power.

"Listen, I know about your grandmother and what a wonderful granddaughter you are. But you owe us quite a bit of money, so spread your damn legs and earn some cash."

Lilly didn't know what to say.

"Come back to work and you won't have to deal with me unless we have a problem."

"It's not for me anymore."

"You really believe that? If nothing else, you need the money to pay back what you owe. No one put a gun to your head and made you borrow it, but they might if you don't pay it back."

Lilly stood up ready to leave.

"Not so fast, Lilly. Sit your ass down and let me finish. Fucking for money has been in style for years and it's never going to go away. There are always men looking for a good lay and interesting conversation and they're more than happy to pay for it. So forget about all the reasons why you aren't going to do it, and just do it. Enjoy the perks while you're at it. You're obviously not getting what you need being a doctor. If nothing else, think of your grandmother."

"Fine. You're right. Give me new clients. I'll make them happy."

"I'm sure you will." Elizabeth smiled. *I knew the grandmother was her Achilles' heel. I love it when I'm right!*

Missing Sam

Every night since Rayna's death Lilly couldn't help but wonder why the puzzle just didn't fit together. That was why she'd had so many sleepless nights lately. She just kept thinking about all the things she knew and trying to fit them together so they made sense. It was pointless, since she got the same result every time, but she couldn't stop herself.

Morning seemed to come just as she fell asleep — same had for so many days. She showered, sipped a cup of espresso and threw on a t-shirt and jeans. Her lab coat hid her wardrobe and lately she didn't care much about what she wore or how she looked. She was lost and uncertain about her future and it showed.

The morning rain didn't bother her; she loved walking in the rain, especially when she air-dried her hair and her curls were going to be frizzy anyway. She pushed her bangs away and continued walking, thinking about everything that was going on in her life lately. She was so deep in thought that she almost didn't hear her phone when it rang. She answered on the last ring.

"Sam? Is that you?"

"Yep. It's me, honey. I missed you but I knew you needed some time."

"You're such a sweetie. You always seem to know what I need, even if I don't."

"Are you all right? Why didn't you let me help you?"

"There's nothing you can do. I'm sorry and I'm really glad you didn't give up on me. I just wanted to sort things out. There's a lot you don't know about me."

"We can agree on that. In fact, I don't know *anything* about you other than you're smart, beautiful and overworked. Don't you think it's time you started trusting me and let me in? You know I love you. Right?"

He loves me? I'm an escort and he loves me... "I promise I'll tell you everything. Soon."

"At least give me something to hold onto 'til then. Please? I'm picking you up for dinner tonight and I'm not taking no for an answer."

She smiled as she neared the hospital. It had been a while since she felt good about anything. When she got to the ER, two of the orderly's were taking a body down to the morgue and Elizabeth was waiting for her. *The bitch just doesn't give up! Everywhere I go she's there.*

Several policemen were talking amongst themselves, but as soon as Lilly came close they fell silent. Suddenly Lilly had a bad feeling. She lifted the sheet covering the body headed to the morgue and gasped. *Oh my God, it's Ben Charles! Shit, this is bad.*

"Hey guys, what happened here?"

"Body was found in the river, floatin' face up. Been there a couple of days."

She did her best to pretend he was just another corpse. "Okay, thanks. You can take him down."

She locked eyes with Elizabeth but then ran off to the bathroom, barely making it to the stall before she threw up. Finally, when there was nothing left in her stomach, she stopped. She splashed cool water on her face, washed out her mouth and then left the bathroom only to find Elizabeth waiting for her.

"You're an emotional little twit, aren't you?"

"Better than being a cold-hearted bitch like you."

Lilly walked past her and headed toward the ER, but Elizabeth grabbed her arm and stopped her. "Listen, this is a bad time for all of us. You're not the only one who was fucking him. There are quite few of us in that category."

"If that's supposed to make me feel better, it doesn't."

"Don't you have patients that need you? Take care of them and forget about Ben."

"Why is he dead and who killed him?"

"When I think you need to know something, I'll tell you."

"Fine." Lilly walked away and didn't look back. *God, I need therapy. I'm too angry and I don't think I'm doing my patients any good. Maybe a professional can talk me through this so I can get back to normal.*

No time like the present. I'd better do it before I chicken out. Lilly opened the crumpled piece of paper she had stashed in her lab coat pocket. It read: Dr. Nicholas Waters, Head of Psychiatry, Memorial North with a phone number. She pulled out her phone and called the number as she walked back to the ER.

Just Like *Pretty Woman*

Lilly probably should've cancelled her date with Sam but she needed to feel something other than sadness. Not only had she lost Rayna, now she'd lost Ben too. *I'm running out of friends pretty quick here. This needs to stop.*

Sam had told her tonight would be her night and he'd be there to fulfill her every wish because she was his queen. He started things out on a great note — three-dozen roses sent to her place.

She was meeting him at the Peninsula Chicago because he knew how she loved the place. Three young male vocalists were standing outside when she got there, singing one of her favorite songs — Whitney Houston's, *The Greatest Love of All.* She couldn't believe it. She felt so special; in fact she almost forgot how bad her day had been.

Making things even more memorable were the many onlookers clapping as the singers finished the song and then watching as Sam kissed her. It was just like the movies. He swept her into his arms and leaned her back just enough so his lips could meet hers. He looked so sexy and she was thrilled she'd decided to keep their date.

"I want you more than I've ever wanted any other woman," he whispered in her ear after he kissed her.

Damn this is exciting, she thought.

There was nothing secretive about this night out. It was like, *Pretty Woman*, revisited. Just like Prince Charming, Sam lifted Lilly in his arms and whisked her away while the singers continued their serenade. The whole thing was surreal.

He put her down when they were standing outside their hotel suite. He opened the door and the lights were dimmed and there were candles flickering everywhere.

No one had ever done anything like this for her before, not even the late Jonah Michaels, and he'd done some pretty terrific things. She often thought about Jonah because he'd always been able to calm her down. *Damn I miss him. I can't lose Sam like I lost Jonah.*

Lilly looked around the room and smiled. Who would ever have thought this small town Ohio girl would be spending the night in the presidential suit one of the most prestigious hotels in the country with such a wonderful man.

She pinched herself to see if she's awake. *I love that he did all of this for me. I think maybe I love him, too. Love? Do I love him? Maybe… He is a sexy stallion.*

They came inside and shut the door. He kissed her passionately and then helped her take off her dress as she unbuttoned his shirt.

Lilly surprised herself when she admitted, "I love you, Sam Sheridan."

"I love you, too. Lilly, please marry me. I don't ever want to be without you again."

Is he the one? I love him but does he love me enough to deal with the real me? Her past continued to haunt her and tonight was no different. Her secrets just wouldn't leave her alone. *If I tell Sam about my past will he still want me?*

She could see how excited Sam was and she didn't want to ruin the mood. *I'll just go with it and see where it takes me. No more negative thoughts tonight.*

It was like the curtain going up on a performance. Tense with an incredibly hard dick he slowly entered her. She liked it slow and steady. She watched him as he watched her; it was hot seeing the desire written on his face.

This wasn't like a typical meeting with one of her escort appointments. It wasn't just sex tonight — it was making love. It was slow and intense but sweet. *I could get used to this,* Lilly thought after they finished.

As they were lying there in each other's arms, Sam blurted out, "I've asked my wife for a divorce."

Lilly was speechless. *Well, that was a mood killer.* "Okay, if we're going to start making confessions, you need to know that I come with baggage — lots of baggage. I'm married, too. His name's Cooper Jameson. I have the divorce papers in my bag, but I haven't signed them yet. I just can't bring myself to do it."

"Everyone has a past. Do you still love him?'

"No. I think I did in the beginning, but his reaction to the way his family treated me slowly at away at that until there was nothing left."

"Then what's the problem? If you love me then it should be easy. Sign the papers and it's over. Then it's just you and me. We could build a wonderful life together."

She didn't answer him but she did kiss him.

Suddenly she began thinking about when she met Cooper. He was strikingly handsome and clearly knew how to use his looks and his family's megabucks to get what he wanted. His dark brown eyes lit up when he smiled and his curly black hair was longer than it should have been — he was irresistible.

Girls were fascinated by his charm and humor so he was used to bedding whoever he wanted. He always had a woman at his side.

She'd had no idea he was such a momma's boy when she married him. He always seemed to respect his parents' wishes, but once they were married things got worse. She could never do anything right — her skin wasn't the right color, her background wasn't fancy enough, and her pedigree was all wrong because her parents were train wrecks. She was not a good fit with Cooper's picture perfect elite black family.

She struggled every day, trying to live up to their expectations. Then, when she lost her daughter in childbirth ... that was really the beginning of the end. She woke up every morning thinking about her baby and she was the last thing Lilly thought about before she fell asleep. What made it worse was Cooper didn't seem to share her anguish over the loss.

All of that is ancient history. Why don't I just sign the damn papers? I've finally found a good man. I deserve a good man, don't I?

Lilly came out of her reverie and said, "Sam, you're wonderful and I love you, but I need to work on me for a while before I can make a commitment to you."

"I think you're perfect just the way you are."

"Well, I don't think that at all. I need to work through some things so I can get on with my life. I've been thinking about therapy for a while now, and you've given me the incentive to go ahead and do it."

Dr. Waters

When Lilly made the appointment with Dr. Waters she wasn't sure if she'd actually be able to go through with it. On one hand she knew she was in trouble but on the other she wasn't sure she'd actually be able to open up to a stranger. *I've got to do something or I'm never going to have the kind of life I want.*

Lilly stood outside the doctor's office, trying to get up the nerve to go inside. *This is the only way I'm going to be able to get myself out of this rut. Come on, Lilly, grow a pair and get in there!*

The office wasn't what she'd expected. It was bright and airy and expensive artwork and several framed medical degrees decorated the walls. Dr. Nicholas Walters wasn't what she expected either. He was a lot younger than she'd pictured when she researched him. He'd had such an impressive resume that she just assumed he'd been practicing for years.

She didn't want to but she couldn't help but notice how handsome he was — dark hair, expressive eyes and a warm smile that immediately made her feel comfortable. She would've been happy to meet him at a bar because then she would be in charge. Being here as his patient was unsettling.

He held out his hand to shake hers and said, "So nice to meet you, Lilly."

"You, too, doctor." She paused for a second, then added, "You came highly recommended."

"That's always good to hear." *She has no idea how good it is to hear that the gossip hasn't tainted my reputation.*

He'd fallen in love with one of his patients and took several months off to regroup and get some therapy himself.

She took a seat on an oversized red leather chair and he took a seat facing her. She nervously assessed the room and realized there was no couch. *I thought all psychiatrists had a couch. How can I pour my heart out from a chair? He'll be looking right at me. What if he doesn't understand the whole escort thing? That's it, I'm not telling him.*

"So, Lilly, what brings you here?"

Lilly took a couple of deep breaths and thought about everything riding on this visit. "Can I be honest with you, doctor?"

"Remember, everything we discuss here is confidential, I don't even tape our sessions," he said, trying to set her mind at ease. *Doctors are always the most difficult patients.* "I'm here to help you, not hurt you. I need the truth at all times or I won't be able to do that."

Lilly smiled, realized she was right about him and began to feel a lot calmer. *Maybe I can tell him everything.* "I actually don't know where to begin."

"It's easier than you think, Lilly. You can't say anything wrong. Just relax and take a deep breath. You don't have to do this all in one day. It's going to take some time."

"This is a lot tougher that I thought it would be."

"I know. Why don't you tell me about the best day of your life and then worst day? That's usually a good starting point."

She waited a few minutes before answering and he allowed her the time to collect her thoughts. "The best day of my life was when I graduated from medical school. I can still remember the feeling of accomplishment I had as I walked up to get my diploma. I was smiling from ear to ear. I'd finally done it. My dream had come true and life was good."

"And your worst day?" Nicholas noted how painful this seemed to be for her. "Just relax for a few minutes. Take your time."

"Umm, well … my worst day was that same day."

Nicholas was surprised by her answer but didn't show it. He waited for her to elaborate.

"I looked out at the audience filled with parents, brothers, sisters, cousins, aunt and uncles, and my heart broke. I was alone. There was no one out there waiting to kiss me and wish me well. My family was all gone, except for my grandmother, and she couldn't be there because she was ill. When my fellow graduates went home to celebrate, I went home and had myself a good cry. Then, I made a promise to myself to never feel that alone again — ever."

What she didn't tell the doctor was that after three hours crying she went to a neighborhood bar, found a sexy guy and brought him home. It was a dangerous thing to do and she decided to never do that again. That was also when she started lying to herself. She decided if she didn't tell anyone about her suffering and how she dealt with it, then it wouldn't be real.

She laughed at herself. *I'm doing all this inside my head when I'm supposed to be baring my soul to this shrink.*

"Care to let me in on the joke? You seem to be enjoying your private thoughts."

"Sure… Why not? That's why I'm here. Right?"

So, she talked while he wrote. She didn't tell him the whole truth; in fact she made up a completely new story and spun the tale.

The doctor wasn't fooled — she wasn't his first reluctant patient. As he listened, he wondered, *Will she ever give in and tell the truth.*

Lilly remained seated after her session was over, rethinking what she'd said. *I made a mistake. If I'm ever going to make a go of this, I'm going to have to tell the truth.* "Hey, can I tell you something before I leave?"

"Sure."

She took a deep breath and then let out her biggest secret. "I'm an escort; I have sex for money. I needed a lot of cash and the quickest way to get it was sex." She blushed and was embarrassed by the admission, but at least it was out there. "Damn, that was hard."

Nicholas smiled. "Fell better?"

"Actually, I do."

"That's good. We have a lot of work to do, but this is a good start."

Lilly smiled. "Nothing wrong with working hard."

After her appointment she went to visit her grand-mother. Lilly smiled when she sat down at her grand-mother's table in the dining room. Nanna was sitting with her regular crew and they were about to have lunch. These people had few visitors, so Lilly was always welcome.

Nanna Laura was looking good. At ninety years old, she was still a beautiful woman. Her white hair was nicely styled, her nails were polished and she was wearing lip-stick today.

Laura's caretaker walked over to the table with Laura's tray and kissed Lilly's cheek. "Hi, honey. She's doing great today. She asked for you this morning. I'm glad you're here."

"Sorry I haven't been here much lately. Work has been crazy."

"She knows that, hon."

Laura took hold of her granddaughter's hand and kissed it. "I love you dear and I know you work hard. Doctors have important things to do."

Lilly smiled. "Yes, they do."

While Laura finished eating, Lilly went to her room and put away her grandmother's laundry. Her closet was filled with beautiful clothes and shoes Lilly had bought for her. She loved to shower her with nice things. *Some-times the good outweighs the bad. I'm going to sell some of my jewelry so she can stay here where she's comfortable and happy.*

Better Late Than Never

Elizabeth and Jake were meeting to have a drink at the Harrington. She had no idea why he wanted to see her. After their last encounter, she never expected to hear from him again. She loved having sex with him because his resistance turned her on. She'd booked a room as soon as he'd asked for the meeting, just in case he wanted to make her a happy woman.

Jake was late and she was irritated, but she stayed. She was having a drink and scanning the room for new recruits. Several of her established escorts had jumped ship after the whole Rayna thing. *Fuck them. There's always other fish in the sea.*

Jake was running late, and all he could think about was how he'd missed Ben's funeral. They'd been partners at the FBI for years and had shared a brotherly bond, so he was busy feeling guilty about not being there one final time for his friend. He felt responsible for Ben's death, even though he knew it wasn't his fault.

Ben's death had been his "a-ha moment," and that's when he'd decided to call it a day with the FBI. He'd realized that if something happened to him no one would be there to take care of his wife. His choice to take early retirement had been the only way he saw to move forward.

Jake didn't want to spend one more minute with Elizabeth than he had to. This was his case and he was going to finish it. Once he arrested Elizabeth, he'd be free. *She has no idea we arrested her cohorts in Buenos Aires and she's next.*

He promised himself that no matter what she tried he wouldn't give in to his sexual desires. *There she is sitting at a table at the back of the room. She looks as beautiful as she ever. Delicious, but mean.*

When she stood to greet him, Jake could tell she wasn't wearing underwear. *This time there'll be no sex for me, but she'll be getting fucked. And this time, she won't like it!*

"Elizabeth you're looking beautiful, as always."

"And you, dear Jake, will look better wearing nothing at all with your dick inside me. You know how I love fucking you."

"After tonight, we won't be meeting again. It's finally over."

"Is that so? How do you figure that?"

"In a few minutes, you're going find out. Just so you know, I never really liked having sex with you." He took a deep breath and smiled. It was like playing Monopoly and he'd just drawn the "Get Out of Jail Free" card.

"I'm the one who says when it's over, not you. Those are the rules. You know that."

"Not this time." Jake grabbed her wrist. "I have enough info on you to put you away for years. We know Rayna wasn't the one running the drug ring — it was you. You fooled everyone — including your husband — for a long time. But that's over now. Did you really expect to get away with it?"

"You must have some bad informants. I'm strictly legit. My husband is a very sick man. Why bring him into this? "

"That's what happens when you marry a bitch. He should have been more careful."

"What the fuck are you talking about? Let's finish this upstairs. I got us a room."

"We won't need a room tonight."

Suddenly the only people in the bar the bar were staff, Jake and Elizabeth.

"Lilly had your husband's blood tested."

"So what? He's had lots of blood tests."

"This time we tested for poison. It was way off the charts. Seems like every night you gave him just a little more so it would build up in his system slowly. That way his decline was gradual and you thought no one would suspect anything. You're one a smart cookie, but you messed with someone smarter than you this time."

"You're fuckin' crazy. I'm leaving."

"Sit down. You're not going anywhere. We know you've been at the hospital every day. You paid the staff who helped you poison him well, but they gave you up in return for immunity."

He could see the rage in her eyes as he continued. "Lilly thought it was strange that you were at the hospital every day. At first she thought you were watching her but she figured out you were there for another reason. She talked to us about it and we found your weak link. I guess some people will do anything for money. I'm sure you paid her well."

"You've got nothing on me. Who the hell would believe a doctor turned hooker?"

"They'll believe me," Rayna said, as she entered with three FBI agents. "Poison, how creative. Poor Oliver, he never saw it coming. Love can do that to you."

"Rayna? What the hell? I thought you were dead!"

"Did you think you could get away with having me shot? You were supposed to be my friend. You didn't even shed a tear at my funeral. You're a cold, heartless bitch."

"I suppose Ben isn't dead either," she said in a matter of fact way.

"Regrettably, his death was very real," Jake said, looking at Elizabeth with disgust.

"When Ben and I put the pieces together, everything pointed to you," Rayna said. "I fought like hell to stay alive so I could put you away for the rest of your miserable life. I think you've hurt enough people."

For the first time ever Elizabeth had no come back.

"I'm a tough old broad and I survived."

"Rayna, you have to believe me. I don't even know how it all began. Once it did, I couldn't stop it."

"Of course you could've stopped it. Why get into drugs? You have money, a husband, property — you had it all."

"Depends on your definition of all. You can never have enough money or power. You were satisfied with same old same old, but not me. I liked the power. Power is the ultimate rush, even better than sex. "

Elizabeth looked at Jake. "Did you really mean what you said? You didn't enjoy what we had?"

"Yes, I meant it. You repulse me," he lied as he watched the three agents move in to cuff her. "Don't forget to read her rights. We don't want her getting off on a technicality."

Handcuffed and struggling, Elizabeth moved closer to Jake and spit at him before they dragged her out.

He wiped his face and smiled. "I'm not sure I've ever felt this good about putting someone away."

"Keep smiling, asshole. I'll be out soon. Nothing can stop me!" she shouted as the agents dragged her out of the room.

Lilly was standing in the doorway. She didn't say a word, she just watched as things went down. Rayna motioned for her and she ran to Rayna's outstretched arms. "I've never been happier to see anyone in my whole life! I can't believe you're alive. I never thought anything Elizabeth said about you was true. I'm so glad she's getting what she deserves. Do you think the charges will stick?"

"I certainly hope so."

Rayna stroked Lilly's hair. "There's someone who wants to talk to you," she said as she handed Lilly a key. "Get out of here. He's waiting. It's penthouse time for you, honey."

"You're kidding. Who is it?

"Just take the key and stop asking so many questions."

The elevator door opened and there was Sam, waiting for her. He looked so handsome and she couldn't believe he still wanted her. She was thrilled to see him but needed to set some things straight. "We need to talk."

"Nope, not right now. I need to kiss you first."

"I just wanted to let you know I signed the papers."

Sam smiled. "Okay. My turn. My divorce will be final soon too. Once it is, we can be together and nothing can stop us."

He put his arms around her and kissed her like she'd never been kissed before. She never imagined her life could change so quickly, but she was confident she'd finally found the man of her dreams.

She remembered her grandmother's advice, "Live and love like there's no tomorrow, and above all else be happy."

The End

Find the Author here:

www.ljsinclair.com

Email: authorladyjanesinclair@gmail.com

Twitter: @authorladyjane

Facebook: Ladyjanesinclair
and ladyjanesinclairlovestyle

www.ingramcontent.com/pod-product-compliance
Lightning Source LLC
Chambersburg PA
CBHW020529120726
47904CB00003B/1018